MW01595722

ISBN: 13:978-1530090525
ISBN: 10;1530090520

DEDICATION

We feel blessed to have the love and support of our children and grandchildren through our personal and professional endeavors. You make our lives complete.

ACKNOWLEDGEMENTS

We appreciate the encouragement of readers who anxiously awaited our second book. You help to drive our efforts and foster our love of writing.

CHARACTERS

Students

- ❖ Brianna – new this year; 12th grade
- ❖ Shawna – friends with Austin; 9th grade
- ❖ Raianna – straight A student; 10th grade
- ❖ Jason – 11th grade
- ❖ Winston – 12th grade
- ❖ Tuscon – new student; 12th grade

Adults

- ❖ Miss Corrina Morgan – Linguistics teacher and head chaperone
- ❖ Mr. Don Barardi – Boys' basketball coach; teachers P.E. and Health; easy-going; wife is named Marina
- ❖ Miss Stacey Tichnell – teaches Biology; helpful with school projects; is not married
- ❖ Mr. Kyle Sutton – teaches Social Studies (World History); is pleasant; is not married
- ❖ Mrs. Vanessa Walker – teaches Consumer Science; married with no children; seems unhappy
- ❖ Dr. Barry Pierce – Principal of National High School; married
- ❖ Trenton Bosco – European government agent

CHARACTERS
(From *The Last Bus: Time Matters*)

Students
- ❖ Austin – hero in previous book; 10th grade
- ❖ Darius – 9th grade
- ❖ Jessica – organized and meticulous; 11th grade
- ❖ Max Sterling – board member's son; 9th grade
- ❖ Melanie Swiger – cheerleader; 11th grade
- ❖ Celeste – a thinker; 11th grade

Adults
- ❖ Mark Rollins – Previous Principal of North Middle School
- ❖ Harman C. Bernard – Superintendent
- ❖ John Sterling – Board member
- ❖ Liz Rollins – wife of Mark Rollins
- ❖ Jo Lee – kidnapper in previous book

CHAPTER 1

It didn't seem like the right thing to do, and according to her grandmother, if it didn't feel right, then more than likely, it wasn't right. But that didn't stop her this time. Later she recalled that it had started during the evening of March 15th. She remembered because it was the Ides of March. Her day on March 15th was different than Julius Caesar's back in 44 B.C. He hadn't survived to see the 16th of March, but she had.

She remembered the time that evening when the phone rang, because American Idol was starting. It was eight o'clock, and she had on her comfy flannel pajamas and fuzzy slippers. Her cat, Abbaryssa, was curled up beside her. She was sitting on the couch with her laptop, ready to begin grading electronic papers that her students had submitted that day, when the phone rang. Her cell phone was across the room on the bench inside the front door where she had left it along with her keys when she had gotten home.

She remembers the details. She had sat down on the couch. The introduction music for American Idol came on. The phone rang. She stood up to answer the phone and when she turned to put her laptop on the couch her arm hit her glass of water, causing it to spill on the floor. She reached the phone when it was still ringing. The cat went running from the spilled water. Corrina answered with her usual, "This is me," but heard only silence. Assuming that she had missed the call, she started to push the button to end the call. But then she heard it. The silence was better than the voice that eerily said, "You should be afraid."

She sat waiting for more, but only heard a click. There was only a blank screen. No number. There was no way to know who that was. Still lost in her own thoughts, she automatically checked to see if she had locked the front door.

It had given her a lot to think about since she was a teacher at National High School, where students now attended who had been kidnapped from North Middle School and taken on a school bus to an abandoned mansion and held for five million dollars ransom. Understandably, security had been extremely tight in their school district after that, and students had been highly protected, which meant that field trips were analyzed and scrutinized for safety and a clear purpose. But that was three years ago. Funny how people forget and other things take precedence, and you're right back to where you were before, when everyone believed that bad things only happen somewhere else and to other people. How quickly the fear and terror and reality are forgotten. That's where we are now.

Corrina Morgan teaches multi-cultural language classes to students at National High School. Students in all grades take her linguistic classes and, in fact, wait sometimes several semesters before getting into her classes. Because she is an engaging teacher, students are excited and enthusiastic about being there each day and always look forward to what might come next. This semester what is coming next is a trip to Italy.

And now for Corrina this is the thing that didn't seem right. Since someone called to tell her that she should be afraid, she might want to reconsider taking the students on the trip. There really might be something she should be afraid of, and maybe she should follow her intuition that told her there could be some danger involved in taking twelve students out of the country. But so much planning – months of effort and fundraising – had led them to where they are now.

Besides, this is different than the intuition, the gut instinct, she had when she was a high school student herself and had felt like she should not go to a party where she had heard there could be drugs. She didn't go, thank goodness, but many bad things had resulted from that party, and the only satisfaction that she had afterwards was that she had not been arrested or had to endure the consequences that others had from being there – like being grounded by parents and going through withdrawal from drugs that were put into drinks.

And then there was the funeral that they were much too young to have to experience for one of their high school peers who did attend that party and did not survive the drive home to talk about it. Corrina had learned at that young age after that experience to follow those gut feelings.

It had helped her on other occasions, like when she was in college and went out into a dark parking lot and felt like someone was watching her. She had returned to the building where she had just completed a night class and waited until there was a group of students leaving the building together, and then got in her car to go to her dorm. However, the next morning there was news all over campus about a girl who had not been so fortunate, and whose body had been found in the bushes beside that same parking lot.

Not long after college graduation, her instinct had protected her from renting an apartment in a building because it just didn't feel safe, and the third-floor apartment she had been interested in didn't even have a fire escape – no means to get out if the unthinkable happened. And it did. Three months later that entire building burnt to the ground with fatal results. Her instincts had saved her again.

Now here she was again with the feeling that something just didn't feel right. But, unlike the other times in her life, she would not follow her gut feelings. She knew that those who had put so much effort into the plans for this trip would never understand her sense of anxiety. They would say she was paranoid and was being ridiculous to even suggest that they shouldn't take a trip that had been planned and saved for all year. So, Corrina put aside her better judgment, checked the front door again, and sat down to grade papers as American Idol continued. She kept her concerns to herself.

CHAPTER 2

Although she didn't discuss her increasing concerns with anyone else, in her mind the concerns still existed, but that would not stop the events from unfolding as they would. The last day of school for students was this Friday. They would be leaving next Monday for Italy, which gave her very little time – really only two days – to finish getting ready to be gone for three weeks. Packing was just one of the many things that needed to be finished. There was also submitting grades, reminders to the students and chaperones who were going on the trip about what to take and not take, and where to be at what time, checking again with the neighbor about getting her mail and taking care of her cat, and saying good-bye to her parents and family. All this before finally meeting up with twelve students and four other chaperones at six o'clock Monday morning at the school to board the bus that would drive them to Dulles International Airport in Washington, D.C. Then, maybe when everyone was there and everything had been taken care of, she would be able to shake this ominous feeling that kept entering her head.

We've made it this far without anything

happening, was a thought that she used to replace the concerns, but then sometimes she would feel like she was tempting fate to say that. She could envision an unidentifiable person with a sneer on his face saying, well, you may have made it this far without anything happening, but I'll show you. All this would run through her mind in an instant with the same result – continuing to pack and prepare to be gone for three weeks.

By Sunday night she had everything ready with her comfortable outfit hanging on the closet door in preparation for the many hours she would be sitting on an airplane. Her alarm was set for four o'clock, which would allow time for a shower and a granola bar and enough time to get to school before six o'clock to check everyone in and help with organizing the luggage for the bus ride to Dulles. What she was not prepared for was the phone call that came in as the eleven o'clock news was beginning. Her purse with her phone in it was on the dresser, so she was able to answer it quickly.

Immediately a hoarse and obviously disguised voice said softly, "I told you that you should be afraid, but you're not listening." Before the click she had time to say, "Who is this?" This time she quickly went to her Call Log and called the person back, although once again no number was visible. There was also no answer, as she predicted.

Now sleep would be impossible. She again checked the doors with the cat following closely behind her. Then, with no other choice – it was too late to call anyone for advice or opinions – she sat on her bed and leaned back against the headboard and thought way too much.

Was it just a coincidence that the caller contacted her just hours before their flight to Italy? While people knew, of course, that there were seventeen from National going on an extended field trip to Italy, there was no particular reason to think that anyone had any motive for not wanting them to go or for threatening to harm any of them. She just needed to relax and try to sleep. As she dozed off sitting up with the lights and TV on, her thoughts turned into a nightmare in which she was running from some unknown person or thing.

It was not unusual for her to have this nightmare. It was a recurring one for her. What was unusual this time was that it was foretelling what was soon to be.

CHAPTER 3

The local news had begun back in March to cover the story of this high school trip to Italy, but last evening had a follow-up story since they were now ready to leave. The national news that picked up on the story in March reminded viewers of the story three years ago in which some of these same students had been involved and the positive outcome that that had led to the arrest of more than just the four adults who directly participated in the kidnapping of twenty students.

Several other adults had been arrested as the ring-leaders of the kidnapping and threats. The news had recapped the students being reunited with their families and again showed the bus being drug up out of the woods. Mug shots were shown of those arrested. They weren't particularly flattering pictures of Stewart, Raole, Marta, or Jo Lee. The newscaster called the student named Austin a hero, but was quick to point out that the principal of the middle school, Mark Rollins, had been relieved of his position as principal.

One person watching was quite interested back in March when the trip was first discussed on the national news and anxiously watched the news last evening when they showed the students from earlier this week having a meeting after school to review their itinerary. There, right in the middle of everything, was that kid Austin. He just looked so smug even three years later. If you looked very closely you could see the itinerary that one group of students was holding up and the details of the map being held by another group of students. And in this age of efficient technology, if you stopped the DVR, you could actually read the itinerary and follow the map that was so nicely color-coordinated to match the itinerary. Each location with the time was clearly outlined.

If you were very clever and resourceful, you could manage to have printed versions of both the itinerary and map. And if you were very clever and revengeful you just might decide to make use of modern technology to suit your own needs. It just so happened that one viewer was very clever and revengeful and found all this very interesting and extremely helpful, and as the news ended, could have been heard to say, "Destination Italy" had anyone been listening.

CHAPTER 4

Despite the shortness of the night, Corrina felt invigorated and excited as she finished putting her makeup into her luggage. Her cat, Abbaryssa, definitely suspecting there was something different happening, wouldn't leave her side and kept entwining herself around Corrina's ankles when she stopped moving. Now gathering her bags, Corrina gently patted Abbaryssa as a farewell gesture before closing the door firmly behind her. She was right on schedule. Nothing eventful or concerning had happened. A fleeting thought was, "See. There was nothing to worry about. The phone calls were just making me feel paranoid."

It was five fifteen in the morning and dark, but thankfully not raining as she drove the twenty minutes on Interstate 295 leading to National High School. Since it was summer, the adults who drove their cars to the school would be leaving their vehicles in the school parking lot for the three weeks they would be gone on the trip. She wasn't the first one here for the six o'clock departure time.

A few cars were already in the lot and a few anxious parents were waiting with students on the sidewalk in front of the school. She had hoped she would be the first one there with time to spare to collect her thoughts and have her papers ready for checking off students and chaperones.

"Ciao, Miss Morgan!" Jessica greeted Corrina, who responded with "Buon giorno!" to encourage the more formal greeting for their visit to Rome.

"Hi, Miss Morgan." Not yet ready for switching to Italian, Melanie greeted Corrina with her usual enthusiasm.

"Hello, Melanie. Are you excited for the trip?" responded Corrina. There would be time enough to remind all the students of the need to communicate in Italian when they would land in Milan.

"Sure, Miss Morgan. I've looked forward to this trip for almost three years," replied Melanie. Although still the enthusiastic cheerleader, Melanie remembered well the trauma they all had felt as middle-schoolers being kidnapped from their school and driven in a bus to an abandoned mansion. However, being a high-spirited person who refused to let anything get her down, Melanie still surrounded herself with positive people and was constantly cheerful.

Next to greet Corrina was another student who had been part of the traumatic kidnapping three years previously. Austin had been considered the main hero who had saved the twenty students from whatever or whoever had intended to harm them.

Now a sophomore at National High School, he was still viewed as an independent individual who definitely had a mind of his own. The fear of him, however, had been replaced with quiet admiration. Some were still wisely wary of what Austin was capable of, because he truly was unpredictable.

In class Austin might appear to be focused on something far removed from the current topic, but just as quickly he might accurately respond to the teacher's question or ask one of his own that caused the entire class to think differently about an issue. It was just almost impossible to second-guess his thought pattern at any given time, but one person seemed more likely than others to understand and be privy to the inner workings of Austin. That was Brianna.

Brianna was a quiet, beautiful senior who was new to National High School this year. She had moved to the Washington, D.C. area after tragedy had struck her family when her father was killed while serving in the U.S. Army. Brianna's mother had needed to be close to family during her grief, and so she had moved in with her sister, Brianna's aunt, with Brianna and her younger brother. Brianna appeared to be withdrawn, but in reality she was learning to cope with the death of her father with the strength of someone much older than her seventeen years. What she did miss, which caused her to appear sad, was the friendship of a boy named Rusty, who remained in her hometown of Madison, Wisconsin, in her old high school. But what Brianna was finding in Austin were those same adult-like thoughts that she had admired and adored in Rusty.

Could it be that she was slowly thinking of Austin as being more than just an intellect and fellow member of the Multi-ethnic Language Club? After all, one icy day this past winter, only days after Brianna had just arrived at National High School, Austin had actually probably saved her life, or at least kept her from severe injury.

It seemed hard to imagine now, and even more difficult to explain if you weren't there to see it, because even Brianna still was reluctant to talk about it or even think about it. That's why the students involved never received any consequences or got into trouble for their actions. But Brianna knew. She knew without a doubt who was responsible but had gotten away with it. No one would believe her anyway, because everyone just loved Melanie. Always cheerful Melanie. Always beautiful Melanie. Never-did-anything-wrong Melanie. But Austin knew the truth. He just never talked about it, and neither did Brianna.

On that day it had been snowing outside all morning and the temperature was well below freezing in the D.C area. The sidewalks around the campus of National High School were treacherous as the students changed classes from one building to another. Brianna was rounding the corner of the main building, above an unused stone stairway that led to a basement door below the icy sidewalk. It was not crowded, since most of the students were ahead of her getting to class. Out of nowhere came a shove in the middle of her back that left her scrambling to keep from falling down into the stairwell.

As she attempted to grab the cold metal railing to stop her fall, she saw the blond head of hair and cheerleading jacket with the name of Melanie Swiger on the back of it. It wasn't hard to guess who had shoved her, but it was unbelievable that the one person behind her, who was in the right place at the right time, was Austin.

With the skill of someone who thinks quickly, Austin reached out and grabbed the back of Brianna's coat collar that provided just enough pressure to keep Brianna from the certain bone-crushing fall that could have been fatal. Although badly shaken, Brianna was not hurt, and she continued on the sidewalk going to her next class, as Austin walked past her to go to his class. She hadn't even thanked him. Nothing was ever said between them about the incident, but he knew, and Brianna knew. And Melanie continued to be the beautiful cheerleader that everyone loved and envied and wanted to be friends with.

Brianna could only imagine what caused Melanie to attack her. In her mind she thought it was because on the first day for Brianna at National, Melanie's boyfriend, Ben, had been assigned as Brianna's student mentor and guide to help her transition to the new school. She guessed that Melanie got jealous of Brianna walking with Ben and asking him questions and texting him for information. That shouldn't make even a girlfriend angry enough to hurt someone, but Brianna knew that there was definitely something sinister below the surface of Melanie Swiger that people didn't see. And now she and Melanie would be in Italy together for three weeks.

CHAPTER 5

Within only a few minutes after six o'clock a.m., the students and chaperones were all there, luggage was stored or carried, and everyone was on the bus that would take them to the Dulles International Airport well ahead of their eleven o'clock flight departure time. They would have plenty of time to check their luggage, get through security, eat breakfast or a snack, and wait calmly to board the plane. Corrina already felt obsessive about counting heads – five adults, including herself, and twelve students. In fact, six of the twelve students on this trip were part of the kidnapping three years ago from the middle school. It was as if those students had formed a bond and developed common interests. Maybe the outcome of that experience had left them stronger and more independent, less insecure and better able to tackle new challenges. None of the six students seemed quiet or withdrawn. They were communicative and able to stand up for themselves.

These six students were joined by six others who were excited to study the Italian history and culture while learning to speak the language. This group of students was ideal to travel with to a foreign country. The chaperones, on the other hand, might be a different story. Coach Don Barardi coached the high school's boys' basketball team. He also taught physical education and health classes, and was well-liked by players and students. Don was easy-going and married with three children and a fourth one on the way.

Don's wife, Marina, worked at home as a realtor in her spare time while taking care of her babies aged one, two, and three years. Her personal goal was half a dozen children and then she might consider stopping at six. For now she was quite content with a fourth one due by Thanksgiving. Either gender would be fine with them. They have two girls and a boy, so either one would be fine. She wasn't picky. Her job as a realtor in the D.C. area provided all that they needed regardless of how many babies she had. They could afford whatever the kids wanted. That's why they could be relaxed and content. All was good and easy for them.

On the other hand, Mrs. Vanessa Walker, teacher of Consumer Science, was a chaperone and a teacher who was very trying and difficult for everyone to get along with – parents, students, colleagues, and even her husband. They had no children, and maybe that's why her husband was rarely around. But possibly it was because she was so difficult to get along with. She was a thoroughly unhappy person. Nothing suited her or pleased her.

Even if she would be eating the most scrumptious piece of chocolate cake ever, she would have said, "But it needs ice cream." How sad not to appreciate what was good in life. How can a person go through life being so miserable? Her husband, Brent Walker, was supposedly a truck driver who spent many hours traveling the roads of America making deliveries. But who knew for sure? He could have been anywhere for all the time he spent at home with his wife. Maybe that's why she was so unhappy. Maybe she felt lonely and unloved.

Then there was Stacey Tichnell. Unmarried and anything but lonely and unloved. Inside and outside of the school days and with her work at National High, she was known as one of those people who was loved by everyone. Although teaching Biology, she was in the midst of everything at the school and was always willing to assist with whatever the current project was. So when volunteers were needed to fly off to Italy with a group of twelve students for three weeks, she was the first to sign up. She'd never want to miss this opportunity.

In contrast, it didn't seem to be something that Vanessa Walker would want to do, except that her husband wasn't around and she had nothing else to do for three weeks. But if you didn't like being around people, why would you volunteer to travel thousands of miles across the Atlantic and in another country if you were only going to complain?

Finally, Kyle Sutton, single, attractive, social studies teacher extraordinaire, was as pleasant as Stacey Tichnell. In fact, maybe too pleasant. Corrina might have a tough job of keeping the teenage girls away from Kyle and the boys away from Stacey. Corrina wondered what she was thinking to bring chaperones that she might have to monitor as much as the students.

Of those four adults, Don might be the most predictable. Think about it. How tough could it be to keep a chaperone who was a husband and father of four babies on track and doing his job? On the other hand, keeping Vanessa happy and students detached from Kyle and Stacey, and them separated from each other, could be a monumental task.

CHAPTER 6

"Mi scusi, Miss Morgan," broke into her reverie as they all sat waiting to board the plane. It was Raianna. A wonderfully reliable straight A student.

"Si, Raianna. What can I do for you?" spoke Corrina.

"I wondered if I have time to go buy a book before we get on the plane. The book I brought has already gotten boring, and it's going to be a really long flight. What do you think?" asked Raianna.

Corrina checked her watch before replying. "Si. Yes, you have enough tempo, time. It's still half an hour before we will get on the plane. Just stay aware of the time so that you won't be late for boarding. And it's always good to have someone with you. Maybe Celeste will go with you to find a book." Before Celeste had a chance to agree, Mr. Sutton agreed to accompany Raianna in search of the perfect book.

Before she knew it, Shawna, Celeste, and Melanie all agreed to go with Mr. Sutton and Raianna. Corrina thought, here we go already, as they walked away leaving Corrina and Mr. Barardi to guard all of their carry-on bags, which should never be left unattended in an airport.

Corrina's additional thought was that managing twelve students and four other adults sounded so easy when the trip to Italy was first discussed. She knew that she would have to stay calm and keep everything in proper perspective. Having a pleasant experience and everyone returning safely from the trip were the most important things.

Here she was obsessively counting heads again. There are seventeen of us. Five are off to find Raianna a book. There should be twelve of us sitting here, but there's only eleven. Who's missing? She always found it easier to group them in her mind by gender – a total of nine females and 8 males. Okay. All the adults were accounted for. All the females were where they should be. But there was a male student missing. Maybe not really missing, but also not sitting here with the others. Tuscon. A new student to their high school this year. He was not here with the others.

"Austin, have you see Tuscon lately?" Corrina asked.

"No, Miss Morgan, but I do remember seeing him get off the bus here at the airport. But after that I don't remember seeing him. Do you want me to go look for him?" Austin offered.

"No, Austin. I don't want to have to worry about you, too. I'll try his cell phone," Corrina suggested. It seemed logical, but led only to his voice mail. She conferred with Don Barardi about what to do with the limited time left before the announcement would come for boarding the plane. He left Corrina to go search for Tuscon, who couldn't be far as long as he had come through security.

Surely someone else had seen him after they got off the bus, but of everyone sitting there, no one remembered being with him after the bus ride. Just as she was ready to find an information desk to ask for an announcement to be made for Tuscon, Don Barardi came back toward her with a worried expression on his face. "I found him," he said with little enthusiasm. "He's in the restroom throwing up. I asked him how he feels, but he was vomiting so much that he couldn't answer and he just shook his head. What do you think we should do with him?" he asked Corrina.

She replied, "There's nothing we can do but get him out of the restroom and onto the plane in a few minutes. We have no choice. He has to go with us. Thank goodness there are restrooms on the plane. Go get him, and have him wash his face and come out here to sit with paper towels in case he vomits again. Make sure he has his carry-on bag with him and puts plenty of paper towels in it. I'll start gathering students with their bags now that Kyle is back with the four girls." Always able to make decisions and make things happen, Corrina told the students and other chaperones to gather their belongings, as Don started walking back toward the restroom to get Tuscon.

The first call came for boarding for First Class for Flight 612. Corrina only glanced at Tuscon to know that something was clearly not right with him. He was shuffling toward them with his head down as he walked the short number of steps from the restroom to where they were standing. His expression could only be described as looking pained. His eyes were vacant and his cheeks each had a bright red spot in the middle.

Now that Corrina saw how sick Tuscon looked, she knew he shouldn't get on the plane; not just because of how miserable he felt, but because whatever he had shouldn't be shared.

"Tuscon," Corrina began, "What do you think about staying home since you are sick?"

"No, ma'am. I don't want to miss Italy. This is the chance of a lifetime for me."

"But, Tuscon, you don't look like you feel well at all. I think we should call your parents to tell them how sick you are and let them decide if you should go."

"No, Miss Morgan. I don't mean any disrespect, but my mother would be broken-hearted if I missed this trip. She worked a second job all year so we'd have the money for the part we had to pay to be able to go. All that work and money would be wasted if I didn't go."

Between holding his stomach and shortness of breath, it was difficult for Tuscon to keep discussing how he felt, but it was clear that Tuscon would be greatly disappointed if the decision were to be made by someone else for him to stay behind.

Mr. Barardi attempted to intervene. "Tuscon, let's think about this together. What happens if you get there and you're in a foreign country and you become really sick? Being sick in a hospital in a different country would be a miserable experience.

Your mother wouldn't even be able to come visit you, and you'd have to wait in Italy until you were well enough to travel back to the United States. What would happen then?"

But, Tuscon only heard about half of that fine speech before he ran back to the restroom with his hand covering his mouth.

Corrina Morgan and Don Barardi looked at each other, but said nothing. Corrina reached into her bag and pulled out the emergency contact list with one hand while pulling her cell phone out of her pocket with the other. She knew she was in charge and had to make a decision and she knew what she needed to do. She stepped away from the group and dialed Tuscon's home phone number. It was the first number listed for him, but there was no answer and no answering machine picked up.

She tried the next number listed for him, but it was disconnected. Corrina tried Tuscon's father's cell phone number, but the recorded message said the mailbox hadn't been set up. She remembered that, according to the paperwork, Tuscon lived only with his mother and sister, so that contact in another state probably wouldn't have helped anyway.

As Corrina walked back toward her group, she again automatically counted heads and was relieved that all were there, including Tuscon, who was now out of the restroom.

He didn't look much better, but he was there. Just in time, too, as the next announcement was made for them to board Flight 612.

CHAPTER 7

Shawna was the first to speak as they walked through the tunnel to enter the plane. "Miss Morgan, can we sit anywhere we want to?"

Jessica answered before Corrina even opened her mouth. "Don't you remember that travel agent telling us about the plane? I know it seems like a long time ago now, but he said that on the plane in whatever class your tickets are in, you can sit anywhere. Do you want to sit together?"

Although an unlikely pair, they began a conversation as they continued together to board the plane. Corrina was again trying to count students and chaperones while trying to mentally process where they were all sitting. She noted that the chaperones had spread themselves out among students as Corrina had requested. Besides the obvious reason for supervising better, some of these students might be a little apprehensive about flying. Although some had been exposed early in their lives to a more affluent way of life, that was not the case for all the students. Several were experiencing air flight for the first time today.

She noticed a few pale and solemn faces as

they stowed their carry-on bags above their heads and found a place to sit. All seemed to be taking the situation as seriously as they had been instructed during their weekly meetings. Paying attention to flight attendants' instructions about seat belts and oxygen masks all of a sudden seemed real to those students who thought it was no big deal when they heard about it months ago while sitting in a classroom.

Now frightening possibilities and the reality of air flight accidents made them all pay close attention to where exits were and securing their carry-on bags, and how to use the oxygen. Maybe students would pay more attention in class if teachers dressed up like flight attendants.

Even Tuscon appeared temporarily engaged, but he was definitely one of the most anxious students. Counting and watching through boarding had replaced Corrina's thoughts concerning Tuscon's illness. Now focusing on him again made her worry about not finding a way to communicate with his parents concerning him being so sick. As she pondered if there had been something else to do, Tuscon managed to hear just the end of the instructions from the flight attendant before moving into and up the aisle as quickly as possible toward the restroom. She felt certain that he was hoping that it was not occupied, and he lucked out this particular time since no one else was even waiting.

The stress of the day seemed to have affected Corrina more than she had anticipated because she thought that she would only close her eyes for a few moments, but she woke up with a start when she immediately realized that several hours had passed. All seemed quiet with most of the students either sleeping or listening through headphones. Still feeling groggy, her eyes again began to close and her mind drift until that feeling wormed its way into her brain. Then, there was no stopping it. Something wasn't right. There was something in her inner mind struggling to surface and get her attention. Then she knew. When she had just glanced around the plane and determined that all was well, she didn't remember seeing Tuscon. She had thought once they were actually on the plane she wouldn't need to be concerned about where the students were. After all, there was nowhere to go for the hours of flying except on the plane. So, why didn't she see Tuscon?

She stood as if to stretch while perusing the passengers' faces in the semi-darkness of the plane. She moved into the aisle and slowly walked while staring almost rudely as she passed each person. The seat where Tuscon had briefly sat was now occupied by an elderly man. Tuscon was not in either restroom because they were both empty. His frequent absences were wearing on Corrina's nerves. Keeping track of him was becoming a full-time job.

It was difficult to identify specific individuals from behind. She went to the front of the first-class section and started down the aisle while carefully looking into each person's face, which presented an interesting situation since some dozed or had heads down or were half-covered with blankets. Finally, she saw him. How strange he had changed seats and was sitting with a girl that she didn't know. They had their heads together as if conspiring. What was he up to? Corinna walked toward him with the intention of asking how he was feeling, but now face to face and with her mouth just opening, she met his eyes.

In the shadows of the inside of the plane, he looked evil. His eyes were squinted and there was a snarl on his lips. She was speechless as he glared at her. And then, in literally a blink of her eye, she realized that this was not Tuscon. So much about this person looked like Tuscon, but yet, it wasn't him. The same dark hair and dark eyes were his, but this person had an earring through his eyebrow and had a small tattoo on his neck, neither of which Tuscon had. Tuscon's hair was long and usually pulled back in a ponytail. This person had short hair, obviously spiked with a strong gel.

While her mind was racing to find something to say to this person who was staring back at her, the blond female sitting next to him spoke up. "Can I help you?" she asked with a sweetness in her voice.

Corrina was just finding her voice, when she responded, "No, sorry. I thought your friend was someone I knew, but I was mistaken."

The girl replied, "That's okay. We were just getting acquainted," but her voice faded and then stopped as her dark-haired companion turned his glare toward her. Her smile quickly disappeared from her face, and she turned to look out the plane's window beside her. Corrina really had no choice but to move on down the aisle away from the Tuscon look-alike. She couldn't get out of her mind the resemblance to Tuscon, but yet the differences that were so obvious.

Now she needed to find Mr. Barardi to discuss the missing Tuscon so they could decide what to do. It still was difficult identifying passengers in the semi-darkness, but Don Barardi was easily identified from his voice. As usual, he was telling stories and entertaining those around him. He was full of coaching tales from years gone by and always enjoyed sharing them with anyone who would listen. He was fun-loving and people could forget their problems just by listening to him. Now he was just starting a new story, "And one night we were late getting to the school because we were given bad directions. And the ref came up to me just as we walked into the gym, and he said that......"

Corrina was standing beside his aisle seat speaking to him, "Mr. Barardi. I need to talk to you for a minute. It's important."

CHAPTER 8

"Don, we can't find Tuscon anywhere on the plane. I thought a boy up toward the front of the plane was Tuscon, but it wasn't. He seems to have vanished. Would you walk up and down the aisle and look for him before I ask the flight attendants to make an announcement?"

Don looked at her in a confused way as if she might be speaking an unknown language. Then he quietly said, "Corrina, are you kidding? He can't be missing. There's no way off an airplane while it's flying. Are you feeling okay? Do you have a fever? Did you catch what Tuscon has?"

"Don, listen to me. I'm not sick. I just can't find Tuscon. You need to look for yourself if you think I'm confused. It would sure make me feel better if I'm wrong, but I think something has happened to him."

Mr. Barardi slowly stood up in the aisle and began his own search. He first walked toward the back of the plane and, like Corrina, peered into strangers' faces trying to see the face of Tuscon in the semi-darkness.

There was no Tuscon to be found was reported

to Corrina twenty minutes later. He had asked each of their students who was awake if they had seen him. No one had. He had truly vanished in mid-air.

It would only be an hour more before they would land in London for a five-hour layover. They had only one hour to locate Tuscon. Corrina approached the flight attendant who was passing out snacks.

"Excuse me. We can't find one of our students who boarded the plane with us. He may be asleep under a blanket. Could you check for us?"

The flight attendant agreed to make an announcement, which she did fairly quickly. She had no better luck than Corrina or Don Barardi had already experienced. The announcement did serve to wake up more people, but Tuscon did not surface. Everyone seemed to be glancing around. Tuscon was described, but no one yelled out with any new discovery of the missing student.

Corrina took a moment to assess her concern. This was ridiculous. He couldn't have gotten out of the plane. He was here and she knew it, but without seeing him, she needed to take the next step, which meant reporting her worries to authorities.

She again approached the flight attendant, who then spoke with the pilot. The decision was made that when the passengers disembarked from the plane in London, the plane would be completely checked before reporting a missing student. Because they were now out of the United States, international law would be followed.

Over-reacting would not be smart. Being

thorough would be necessary and wise before involving the law. She would wait.

The next hour did not pass quickly, nor did it provide any sightings of Tuscon. As they landed in London, the students and chaperones gathered their carry-on bags and belongings. Their luggage would automatically be transferred to the plane going to Milan, Italy. It appeared that everyone had everything they came with, except Tuscon. Corrina went to where Tuscon had stowed a carry-on bag, but the space was empty. She glanced around at other compartments, but they were also empty.

Corrina had no choice but to get off the plane. Everyone else seemed pre-occupied with their own concerns and demands, but her responsibilities were just beginning. She approached the closest help desk inside the terminal to discuss Tuscon and ask if the plane was searched when it landed. It was unlikely that she would find any sympathy or concern when it was impossible to explain, but she had no choice. She began the difficult task of explaining how a student had entered the plane, but didn't get off of it when they had landed.

"Could you repeat his name, please," stated the terminal representatives at the desk.

Again Corrina repeated the spelling of Tuscon Lacardio. At first she was confused by their lack of concern, but shortly it all began to make sense when one of them looked up from the list and said, "Did you say Tuscon Lacardio? Miss Morgan, is this some kind of a joke? He disembarked from Flight 612 with the rest of your group and even checked with us about the time your next flight would be going to Italy. Are you a chaperone?"

Corrina stared while processing this information. It was impossible. They all had searched and made announcements. Now what?

Without further discussion, other than a quick, "Thank you," Corrina looked around and walked toward where a majority of their students and chaperones were sitting to wait for the flight that would take them to Milan, Italy. Don Barardi sat with the group from National High.

Corrina approached him while asking, "Have you seen Tuscon?"

Don said, "We think we saw him from behind after he got off the plane. He had to have been somewhere on the plane all the time we were looking for him."

Corrina had her doubts about all of this being true. Something was still not right. "But where is Tuscon now?"

Kyle Sutton answered for Don Barardi, "I guess in the restroom," since Don's attention seemed to be drawn to something happening between two students in a few rows behind them.

Corrina said to Kyle, "Did you actually see him go into the restroom?"

Kyle predicted, "No, but I assume he'll show up again when it's time to get on the next plane."

Corrina attempted to get Don's attention, "Mr. Barardi, what's going on over there?"

Don responded, "Melanie and Brianna seem to be squabbling. I'll go see what's going on."

Don fortunately arrived as the two girls' voices rose loud enough to be heard from a distance as they moved toward each other. Don stepped between the girls, as students began to surround them. Corrina knew that when two girls are involved in a disagreement it was usually over a boy. This would be dealt with later.

Trying to sort out this scuffle, finding food, shopping, and napping seemed to occupy everyone for their five-hour layover until their next flight was called. The two girls had not resolved their differences, but they did go their separate ways to surround themselves with their individual group of friends. Corrina alone wondered about Tuscon being so elusive.

CHAPTER 9

The flight to Milan, Italy, from London was only an hour and a half long. It was short compared to the amount of time it took to fly across the Atlantic Ocean. It barely allowed enough time for counting heads, but, of course, Corrina felt obligated to do it. She had just started locating people after the seatbelt sign allowed passengers to remove their seatbelts. She always felt somewhat reluctant to take off her seatbelt, but it was almost impossible to find everyone if she remained in her seat.

As she moved into the aisle, she glanced forward and saw what looked like Tuscon several rows ahead seated with Celeste. As Corrina began to walk down the aisle, Miss Tichnell stopped her to discuss the plans for when they arrived in Milan. Sitting next to Stacey Tichnell was Brianna, a senior this year at National.

She was the only girl on the trip who was in her last year of high school. Brianna had her heart set on going to Georgetown University next fall, but only time would tell if the scholarship she needed would be awarded to her.

The potential recipient above her on the list

was trying to decide between Stanford University and Georgetown University, but had not decided which side of the United States would be her choice for the next four years of education. Brianna, on the other hand, knew that only a scholarship would get her to Georgetown, but without a doubt, that's where she wanted to go to college.

She had been discussing this with Miss Tichnell when Miss Morgan approached them as she continued her counting of those from National – five adults and twelve students. Brianna was more like an adult than a high school student. She knew what mattered to her in life and was serious about obtaining it. Her one weakness in her entire life occurred this year. His name was Tuscon.

Brianna had fallen madly in love with Tuscon when Austin continued to ignore her. The mystery of Tuscon intrigued her. The newness of all the unknowns about him infatuated her. She wanted to know all of his secrets. She longed to share moments with him away from the world. All of her logical thoughts vanished when Tuscon was near, and she imagined his aloofness toward her would be replaced with warmth if they could spend time together in Italy. She hadn't decided how she could make that happen, but she knew he would become interested in her when the opportunity presented itself. She would do anything to be with Tuscon.

That led to Brianna's question now directed toward Corrina. "Miss Morgan, don't you think it would be a good idea if we were in pairs for our trip? You know, just in case we need something or we get lost or we have trouble with the language, or just anything. And since there are six guys and six girls, wouldn't it make sense to pair us together in a girl-boy pair? Have you thought about that idea?"

Corrina had not considered it, and her thoughts weren't leaning in that direction now. She immediately envisioned a couple being lost in Italy together, and instead of helping each other they would go further astray from the planned itinerary. Her answer was not what Brianna wanted to hear, but Corrina made it clear that each student was expected to do all the right things on this trip according to the plan that had been discussed for the past several months.

Although adult-like in most circumstances, Brianna's expression indicated the disappointment she felt at not being paired with Tuscon. Brianna decided that a different plan would have to be attempted by her.

Meantime, in the short time until landing, Corrina looked for each adult and student from National but was stopped before finishing by the announcement to prepare for landing. Corrina would just have to hope everyone was where they should be and had what they needed to depart from the plane for their first destination – Milan, Italy. Counting heads was especially difficult as everyone was reaching for their carry-on luggage and moving toward the front of the plane.

All were a little nervous, but none so anxious as Corrina. She felt the weight of the responsibility completely on her, and not for the first or the last time wondered if the outcome of this trip would be what

she had hoped when she had pursued getting
permission from the principal for flying to Italy with a
group of students and adults.

CHAPTER 10

The Milano Malpensa Airport is the largest of three airports in Milan, Italy. With the six-hour time change between Washington, D.C., and Milan, the nine hours in the air and five hours waiting in the London airport for their flight to Italy, and the time it took to retrieve their luggage in Milan, they would soon be traveling for nearly twenty-four hours since they had met at the school yesterday morning at six o'clock.

As they would soon be starting on their second day together, needless to say they were all exhausted but exhilarated to finally be in the country of their destination. The travel agent had wisely chosen the Sheraton Airport Hotel, which is inside the Malpensa Airpot in Milan, knowing that they would all feel like going to bed immediately after being up for an entire day and just beginning to feel the effects of jet lag. Although the price of the convenience of the rooms was higher than if they had ridden on the shuttle to another hotel, the cost was well-worth just being able to crash in their own hotel beds.

With all their luggage fortunately located, they were divided into rooms according to the methodical plans by Corrine. The two male chaperones, Don Barardi and Kyle Sutton, would share a room, while the two female chaperones, Stacey Tichnell and Vanessa Walker would be unlikely roommates. This left Corrina Morgan on her own. This wasn't necessarily Corrina's preference, but it was how it needed to be. It worked out well that there were six male students and six female students with two boys or two girls in each room. This made a total of nine rooms wherever they went.

That was a lot to keep track of for Corrina, but that was part of what she knew her job to be. She felt that losing any paperwork that was required or being unsure of where students were at any given moment was unacceptable. Corrina knew ahead of time that this would not be a vacation for her, but she knew she could count on the other chaperones if she needed help.

The male students were divided into three rooms for boys: Max and Darius; Austin and Jason; Winston and Tuscon. The female students were divided into three rooms for girls: Shawna and Raianna; Brianna and Jessica; Melanie and Celeste. Hopefully they were all so tired that falling into beds in their assigned rooms was the only thing on their minds. Corrina knew that's what she planned for them all.

Using Italian to keep them all familiar with the language, Corrina reminded them all that at l'una (one o'clock) they needed to meet in the lobby to go on the tourist tram to their tour of Sforza Castle in Milan. She assured them that this was just the beginning of the excitement in Italy. She watched as they all walked in the direction of the elevators and crowded in to go to their rooms.

She knew the pairs selected as the roommates might not be the ideal situation, but these were the students who wanted to be here, and she firmly believed that if you worked hard enough at it you could enjoy the time with anyone. It shouldn't take a crisis like a kidnapping in middle school to expect that people could share the same space and get along.

It seemed that all went well enough and everyone settled into their rooms and were content. That was from Corrina's perspective in her own room. She was only hoping that things were going well in all the other rooms. It was only the beginning of their exciting time together in Italy – but maybe not the kind of excitement that Corrina had planned on. How naïve of her to believe that everyone was tired enough to just sleep.

No one knew a lot about Winston. He had entered National High this year as a senior. He had enough credits to graduate with his senior class this year, and had earned the money to go on this trip. Although he was now technically not a National student since he had already graduated, he was still permitted to be on the trip and was expected to follow all the same rules as every other student. He had agreed to that and everyone expected that to happen.

Now he was paired with Tuscon as roommates for the trip. Since he had always indicated that he was a responsible student, Corrina thought that he would be a good influence on Tuscon. It wasn't that she doubted Tuscon's responsibility, she just had a feeling, a concern, about him. It was that same feeling that had plagued her initially about something not seeming to be right. However, except for his unexplained illness and mysterious absence on the plane, she had nothing to base her feelings on.

So tonight would be a test to find out what could happen between these two students who had only gotten to know each other during this year in the linguistics class. Guys are different. They seem to get along without having to build a friendship, unlike girls who seek to have something in common and seem to need something in common to have a friendship before getting along. So here were Winston and Tuscon paired together but seemingly fine with it.

With their door barely closed, Winston was the first to speak. "So, Tuscon, what would you like to do in this fine city of Milan for the next few hours?"

Tuscon looked perplexed for only a second before replying, "I think we need to get out of this room and see what's happening downstairs in the lounge. What do you think?"

"Sounds good to me. Let's go. Do you have your room key?"

Tuscon held up the card that would get them back into their room and started for the door. Winston was right behind him.

CHAPTER 11

Two eighteen-year-old American males had no trouble getting beer in the hotel lounge. What they hadn't counted on was that Don Barardi and Kyle Sutton had also been restless and not ready to settle down and relax in their room, and also sought the comfort of the lounge to unwind. So the shadow crossing the boys' table in the subtle light of the candles lighting the room was not a waitress asking them if they wanted another drink. It was Don and Kyle asking them if they were ready to go to their room and sleep it off. And just to be sure they would get the answer they wanted, they each put a hand under the elbows of Winston and Tuscon as they guided them to their feet.

Immediately Tuscon became defensive and jerked his arm away. Winston, on the other hand, was more than willing to cooperate. He realized that he had been caught breaking a rule.

Tuscon, however, was ready to fight about it. He said loudly, "Get your hands off me. I'm technically an adult and can do whatever I want. What are you going to do about it? Kick me out of school? I'm not going to be back anyway!"

Making a scene was not the intent. Getting Winston and Tucson to leave quietly and go to their room was what Don and Kyle planned when they saw the boys in the lounge. That didn't seem to be what was going to happen. Tucson seemed intent on fighting with them even to the point of aggression. What to do to maintain Tucson's dignity but take charge of the situation was now Don's purpose.

With a strategy in mind to let go of Tucson in order to face him to try to reason with him, he failed to see Tucson's fist coming at him. It's one thing to verbally assault a teacher, but to physically assault a teacher created a whole different scenario. Kyle reacted immediately and moved behind Tucson to lock his arms around Tucson's chest while pulling him away from using his fist again. Despite an already swelling eye, Don moved to the side of Tucson to assist if needed.

By now waiters in the bar were paying attention to what was happening. At first they seemed hesitant to become involved, but it was difficult for them to ignore the fact that Tuscon was struggling with Kyle while Don was attempting to help and trying to avoid Tuscon's swinging arms. But since being a waiter even in a hotel lounge in Italy affords few chances for excitement, the waiters converged on the struggling student and easily put him on the floor with one of them kneeling on the small of his back as he lay face-down on the hardwood floor.

This is when familiarity with another language is extremely helpful when you're traveling in another country, even for chaperones. The waiters were asking questions in Italian way too fast for either Don or Kyle to grasp what either were saying. Their blank stares must have given the three waiters a good enough hint that there was a language barrier because all three began speaking English at once. Don was the first to try to answer above Tuscan's yelling.

"We are here on a high school trip. He is one of our students. He shouldn't have been drinking and so we were trying to escort him upstairs when he hit me."

The waiters at first seemed slightly confused. They questioned the word 'escort.' One of them said, "What is escort?" Don was the first to answer, "We want them to come with us upstairs to go to their rooms."

Although immobile on the floor, it didn't stop Tuscon from yelling, "You need to leave us alone! I'm going to sue all of you for violating my rights as an American citizen!"

While the waiters may not have understood the word "escort," they seemed to easily understand the word "sue." With a nod from one of them to the other two, they got off Tuscon and backed away saying, "Our pardons. We didn't know you were American. You have your rights and we'll leave you alone," as they disappeared through the door behind the bar, obviously separating themselves from further involvement.

Once again Don and Kyle were faced with the dilemma of what to do about Tuscon. Winston, on the other hand, had determined to stand still right where he was and do whatever he was told to do while hoping for a more positive outcome than the expression on Don's face made it seem like might happen. The dilemma solved itself within seconds. As Mr. Barardi and Mr. Sutton stood deciding what to do next, Tuscon was out the door sprinting faster than either could move or think what to do. They both shouted to whomever was within the range of their voices, but there was no reaction to their pleas for help. It was late, and the other patrons in the lounge and people in the lobby didn't seem to want to be involved. And so Tuscon ran out through the front door of the hotel and out into the street and down a dark alley. Neither Don nor Kyle even saw the direction Tuscon turned. He was gone just that quickly out into the streets of Milan, Italy.

CHAPTER 12

Now Don and Kyle were faced with the obvious concern about waking up Miss Morgan to tell her that one of the students had disappeared out into the night. As they delivered Winston to his room with an admonition of consequences that would be discussed later, Don and Kyle debated only briefly that maybe meeting with Corrina could wait until morning, but they quickly disregarded that idea because they knew that the longer Tuscon was out there somewhere the more risk there was to him in an unfamiliar country with limited language skills and inadequate resources.

Don quietly knocked on Corrina's door. He knew that it was unlikely that she would hear his soft knock and inwardly hoped that maybe she wouldn't. But, he knew he had no choice but to knock louder. This time he heard her voice calling out, "I'm coming. Who is it?"

Don knew Corrina well enough to know that she would be cautious about opening her door to someone in the middle of the night without some explanation through the door. However, he felt that this discussion really needed to be done face-to-face.

"Corrina, it's Don. Kyle and I need to talk to you. It's kind of an emergency."

"Okay. Let me get my robe and slippers on."

The word *emergency* seemed to always get a chaperone's attention fairly fast. Corrina opened the door and motioned the men inside. She had decided quickly that whatever the emergency was it should not be discussed in the open hallway in a hotel in Italy surrounded by strangers.

"Okay, guys. What's going on?"

As best he could, given the lateness and the eminent concern, he explained to Corrina what had happened. She visibly cringed when Kyle summed it up with, "And so Tuscon is out there in Milan angry and by himself."

Don verbalized just what Corrina was thinking, "What should we do?"

When you've been up for almost two complete days, you're tired, and frustrated, that might be the time to monitor what you say. Corrina was all of this, but she didn't adhere to her own personal policy of being quiet if in doubt about what might come out of her mouth. "I knew I should have checked more carefully about Tuscon's background. When there was that question about previous violations of the law, maybe I should have looked into it about Tuscon. I should have just not allowed him to come."

Corrina continued and began to sound even more agitated. "I just knew there was something questionable about him. I knew there was something wrong with him or something going on with him. Something just wasn't right. He's been so much trouble ever since we got to the airport. And now look where we are."

It was obvious to Don that she would just keep going if he didn't redirect her. He had never seen Corrina not in control of herself.

Maybe the strain of the trip and already dealing with Tuscon was just more than she could cope with. It appeared that she was overly tired and babbling and would continue without solving the problem if he didn't do something to get her attention.

"Corrina, what do you want us to do to help?"

That simple question seemed to effectively bring Corrina back to reality and into problem-solving mode. She reached for the phone on her nightstand and dialed the lobby.

"Could you tell me the phone number for the local police?"

She repeated, "Police. Polizia. Call the police. Chiama la polizia." She wrote down a number and hung up.

She again picked up the phone, dialed, listened briefly, and then responded, "We have lost a student. A boy. Ragazzo. Not a baby. A young man. Giovanotto. Ran away – scappare – from the hotel."

Corrina's countenance seemed to change even as Don and Kyle watched. They saw how quickly the pitch of her voice and volume rose considerably.

"What? How old? Eighteen – diciotto. Why does that matter?"

Again a brief pause before her response, "He isn't a signori. Not an adult. He's a boy. A student."

Her eyes were raging as she hung up the phone

not very gently. "They said they can't do anything because he's eighteen and they consider him to be an adult. So he has to be missing for several days before they will even talk with us. Now what?"

All three stood quietly with their own thoughts. Corrina was the first to speak. "Tell me what really happened that led to Tuscon taking off into the night alone in a strange city."

As Don and Kyle explained the episode in the hotel bar, Corrina formed her own opinion about right from wrong. She did not herself ever make it a practice to put hands on a student. On the other hand, she could almost see where it was a matter of protection for Don and a means of defense against an out-of-control student. She wondered, though, what might have been the outcome had Don not touched Tuscon initially. Would he have calmly walked with them to his room? She also wondered if Tuscon had only been looking for an excuse to separate himself from the rest of the group. Maybe that had been his plan all along. Even if Don hadn't grabbed his elbow, would he have still bolted from the hotel?

She could continue to speculate, but that was not a productive means to take care of the issue at hand. She got a folder from her carry-on bag and began once again to look up the information about Tuscon.

Using her cell phone this time, she dialed a number. As before, there was no answer and no way to leave a message. Nothing had changed. Now she surmised that this probably was never a means to communicate with someone in his family.

This time she resorted to using additional information that should allow her to be in contact with a neighbor. This was a preventative precaution she took with each student just in case a parent or guardian couldn't be reached. She was pleased that it appeared that someone was answering the phone.

"Hello. My name is Corrina Morgan. I am a chaperone with National High School. We're on a trip to Italy. Your neighbor, Tuscon Lacardio, who is on the trip with us, listed you as a neighbor with whom we could communicate regarding him. Do you happen to know if his mother is at home next door. We have been unable to reach her both times today that we tried. Is there any way……"

Her voice trailed off as she listened to a voice on the other end of the phone line. The look on her face spoke volumes. Don realized immediately that this was not going to be good.

"What? Are you sure? What do you mean you have never heard of Tuscon Lacardio? He listed you as a neighbor. You must be mistaken. Just look out your window and see if you see a car in their driveway."

Again silence as Corrina listened. Her breathing seemed to stop. Neither Don nor Kyle thought it was smart to ask any questions or even move.

Corrina sat on the edge of her bed as she finished the conversation. "You don't even live in a neighborhood? You say you live in an apartment? Are you even in the state of Maryland or Virginia?"

Again what seemed like too long of a silence

before Corrina's voice, now a whisper, could barely be heard saying, "The state of Missouri. And you have no idea what I'm talking about and have never heard of Tuscon Lacardio. Right?"

Her apology was brief, "I'm sorry to have bothered you. Thank you."

CHAPTER 13

The silence seemed to go on way too long. Don and Kyle began to feel uncomfortable. Don didn't know how else to explain what had happened in the hotel lounge that night. It was what it was. Tuscon had gotten angry and had run. As far as Don knew, there was no reason other than escaping a bad situation that Tuscon himself had created. He had no indication for thinking that it was preplanned by Tuscon or that he had an ulterior motive for separating himself from the group. If Tuscon had not been genuinely angry, then he was an outstanding and very convincing actor. Not knowing Tuscon very well, that was possible, but there was no reason to suspect him of any questionable activity.

Don repeated the story once more, which seemed to agitate Corrina all over again. Kyle decided to interrupt the pointless repetition to say, "Let's go outside and look for him. Should we alert the other chaperones?"

It became an immediate plan of action. It was agreed that Don and Kyle would go to the other chaperone's rooms to make them aware of the situation and then meet in the lobby in fifteen minutes to begin the search.

Was Kyle the only person who felt like they were wasting valuable time? Probably not, but they all went through the motions like their plan would make a difference, and within fifteen minutes, as planned, they met downstairs and were joined by an additional chaperone, Stacey Tichnell.

It was decided that Kyle and Stacey would go one way and Corrina and Don would venture in the opposite direction. They would keep in contact through their cell phones. To all four, it felt like a hopeless situation, but doing nothing would seem like they didn't care, and as chaperones none of them considered that to be an option.

They had no way of knowing the whereabouts of Tuscon. They couldn't even predict what he might do because he was an unknown entity. He hadn't grown up in their school system. They didn't know his parents. Even in their large school, there was a sense of community – of belonging and knowing each other's families and backgrounds. When a student moved in, it took a while to establish that rapport and cohesiveness. With Tuscon, that hadn't seemed to happen. Like Winston, they had just seemed interested in the linguistic classes.

It was difficult to get students to be interested in giving up part of a summer, even to take a trip like this. So, if a student expressed an interest and was able to pay the money, no one usually questioned their background or family situation.

Maybe they should have asked. Maybe in this case a little bit of knowledge would have been helpful, or maybe even crucial. But it wasn't done.

And so Tuscon did what Tuscon had always done. He went to a bar and started drinking. It was dark and he blended in with the locals and visitors alike. No one in this bar questioned or cared or even communicated with him – in the beginning. He was content to drink in silence and the scowl on his face warned others to steer clear. He didn't care that he was being looked for. He was done with that whole routine of being somewhere on time and being checked on. He had only used the school system to get where he wanted to be – in Italy, and he wasn't going back.

They should just leave him alone because even if they found him they couldn't force him to do what they wanted. Let them try. He knew what it took to stop people. And in his life he had learned the consequences of hesitation. Now, he wouldn't hesitate to do whatever was necessary.

Apparently here in Italy, or at least in Milan in this bar, they didn't monitor how much a paying customer drank. He just sat there and quietly consumed. As if on cue, a tiny blond entered the bar, looked around, saw what she wanted, and went to sit on the stool beside Tuscon. At first he didn't acknowledge the presence beside him. He continued to drink. From an outside observer's perception, it was all just a coincidence. That perception would be wrong, but the history between them was not obviously visible. Just two people meeting in a bar.

CHAPTER 14

Searching the streets and nearby lounges and pubs seemed senseless, and turned up no clues for the location of Tuscon. They decided at three in the morning, Milan time, to return to the hotel to sleep. They had left a description of Tuscon at nearby locations in case he made an appearance. They just didn't hit the right bar or if they had, they would possibly not have recognized the short-haired tattooed and earringed individual sitting on a stool.

As planned, everyone met in the hotel lobby at one o'clock in the afternoon to board the tram to tour the Sforza Castle in Milan. Corrina had decided that she needed to keep them all on schedule and continue to conduct business as usual despite Tuscon's absence. Students had asked where he was as they boarded the tram, but she was vague with her replies. Apparently the other chaperones weren't volunteering any information either, which was wise since at this point they didn't know any answers. He was just gone and the police didn't care.

Corrina had tried reaching Tuscon's father again according to the cell phone number listed, but again to no avail. Both other numbers listed also had not yielded results. She was once again left without answers regarding Tuscon.

So, despite anything else happening, they were on to the Sforza Castle in Milan with the group. It seemed that the pairs selected by Corrina to be roommates were wise choices because they seemed to have migrated toward each other for this tour. Corrina felt relieved. It was so much easier when dramatic squabbles between students were at a minimum.

Throughout the tour, Corrina would catch a glimpse of her students in various parts of the castle. Knowing that they shared different interests, Corrina had decided it was easier and more beneficial to the students to set a time to meet afterwards rather than attempting to try to keep them together. It seems that the decision was a good one since everyone she saw seemed to be enjoying all that the castle offered.

The Sforza Castle was designed during the Renaissance period in the 14th Century, but had been destroyed and rebuilt. The art museum contained the last masterpiece of Michelangelo, the Pieta Rondanini, which he had been working on only six days prior to his death in 1564. The castle also included frescoes by Leonardo da Vinci, where he had actually worked for twenty-four years.

In the nearby church of Santa Maria delle Grazie was the famous painting by Leonard da Vinci, The Last Supper. Corrina was grateful that Mr. Sutton had covered the Renaissance this year in World History with a special emphasis on the relevance and value of ancient artwork.

The overall calming effect of the castle was

helpful to each of them after the stress of travel and losing Tuscon. The blend of the ancient art and historical musical instruments with a reading room all created a tranquil setting for casually wandering and experiencing culture that made the outside world seem far away.

During the tranquility, Corrina was still attempting to reach Tuscon on his cell phone and his parents on their cell phones without success. She had debated scouring the streets and its businesses surrounding Milan, but she suspected already that she would find no trace. She had no instincts regarding Tuscon, but she did have a feeling about the neighboring area. It seemed that not just the dark of last night, but the entire city, had the ability to swallow up individuals and hide the stories along with them.

There was no denying that Tuscon was truly gone and might never be seen by them again. Or at least alive, depending on who or what might catch up with him first before they did. She had heard distressing stories about students disappearing in foreign countries. She just never dreamed that she would be involved in a scenario like the one enfolding in her life right now.

This was a chaperone's worst nightmare. It was inconceivable to lose a student on a trip. Maybe the phone call months ago had been warning her about this very thing. Maybe someone out there had a plan and they were all becoming a part of it.

As Corrina was reassuring herself that those kinds of things only happen in movies, she briefly remembered the kidnapping of some of these same students only three years ago, but continued with her schedule. She felt this need to follow the itinerary no matter what else was happening.

CHAPTER 15

After meeting all the chaperones and students at the designated location, they went to dinner at El Brellin, a restaurant with pasta and home-made desserts, which overlooked the canal from their table upstairs. It was during the first course that her cell phone rang. As if half-expecting a call, she answered it on the second ring. At first there was only silence on the other end as she moved toward a window to get better reception. Then she heard it. Laughter. Not just any typical laughter, but loud, hysterical laughter with someone screaming, "Are you afraid yet?" Then, nothing. No voice. Just the laughter that seemed to be some kind of message that possibly meant nothing to her. Was it related to Tuscon? The number said, "Number blocked," so she didn't even know what phone the call had come from. When the call ended, she again tried Tuscon's cell phone number, with again no answer and no way to leave a message. She only heard that the voicemail box was full.

She returned to the table and tried to engage in the conversations that had continued while she was away from the group.

It was hardly any use – her mind was

elsewhere wondering and speculating about what was going on. There was a lot to think about.

Lost in her own thoughts, Corrina quietly surveyed the group as they ate and carried on various conversations. Her mind suddenly focused on Austin. She had not given him much thought, but the serenity of these moments created time to reflect on his heroism with the middle school kidnapping. Why was she not seeing any concern from him for Tuscon?

He didn't seem a bit ruffled about a missing student. Where were his thoughts tonight? What she did notice was Austin talking with Shawna. Then she put it all together. The look on his face made her realize that thoughts of Tuscon were not his greatest concern. Apparently thoughts of Shawna were a little more important to his male adolescent brain right now.

Seeing their oblivion to anything going on around them put a smile on Corrina's face. "Young love," she reasoned, and sighed. But, ever the chaperone, her next thought was that Austin and Shawna together would probably need to be closely monitored. Her next thought was, oh gosh, I'm getting old before I should. Let them just enjoy life and I'll keep hoping for love for myself like that.

She noticed that Mrs. Walker looked somewhat lonely and bored with no one talking to her. The other chaperones, Don, Kyle, and Stacey, were busy discussing some changes in football rules for the upcoming season. The students were all having engaging conversations that were meaningful to them. That left Vanessa Walker on her own.

She didn't look like she minded, but Corrina

knew Vanessa well enough now to know that her outward facial expression rarely changed, so there was no way to guess what she was thinking.

Corrina decided to join Vanessa on the empty chair beside her. They hadn't had a real opportunity to talk to each other since school was out. "Hi, Mrs. Walker. May I sit here?"

Corrina detected an ever-so-slight glimmer of being pleased that Corrina had taken notice of her. Mrs. Walker's response was not altogether friendly, but still seemed like a genuine step toward friendliness, "Only if you call me Vanessa. I feel old when I'm called Mrs. Walker outside of school. Although I am old enough to be your mother, please call me Vanessa. Since we're travelling together for three weeks, we can at least act like we're friends."

Somewhat taken aback by Vanessa's response, Corrina was still pleased that she had elicited some communication from Mrs. Walker, and willingly chose to ignore the possible sarcasm embedded within it. "Sure, Vanessa. Have you enjoyed the trip so far?"

Corrina could understand why the students often commented about how serious Mrs. Walker was as Vanessa turned toward her with the same unreadable expression before answering, "Well, it has been an interesting trip so far, to say the least. With all the excitement brought about over Tuscon, it's hard to say whether any of us have enjoyed our trip. What's your best guess about what he's up to?"

Unsure of how to answer, Corrina knew she sounded vague at first, and then became more straight-forward, "I think he's possibly scared. Probably he's angry. Maybe he's lost."

Vanessa's response left little room for doubt about what she was thinking. "Let's be realistic. Maybe he's working hard at making you think he's lost. I don't think we'll ever see him again. We'll never know if he's dead or alive. And that's the way I think he wants it."

CHAPTER 16

The next day in Milan, with now eleven students and five adults, their total of sixteen people could be divided into two groups of eight that met the limit for guided groups. Although none of them had ever been on a Segway, the guide gave them lessons before setting off on their three-hour tour through Milan. The guide spoke to them throughout the tour through their individual headsets.

The weather was perfect and the spirit light as they glided past Sforzesco Castle, Piazza Duomo, and a gallery dedicated to the King of Italy. The guide was speaking English and they all felt fortunate that they didn't have to translate from Italian and that Miss Morgan had familiarized them well with the sights they were seeing so that they could relax and enjoy the tour. It was difficult enough for them to concentrate on riding the Segways without toppling off into the streets of Milan. Corrina also felt like she could relax since the five chaperones were divided between the two groups.

She didn't feel completely responsible for everyone when Don and Vanessa could easily stay with the other group and monitor six students. She felt more relaxed and less stressed than she had been since leaving Washington, D.C.

As happens in life, just at the time you feel like you can stop wondering what bad thing will happen next, is the exact time that something happens. It's like tempting fate to even think that everything is going well. Such was the case, but Corrina didn't even know. She was completely unaware of the darkly dressed figure lurking in the shadows of the next alley they would pass. Even in the bright sunlight, the dark within the alleys could not be penetrated, especially by people who were concentrating on staying upright and could barely glance to the right or left as they sailed by.

That's what made it so easy to step out without warning into the path of a moving Segway, causing the occupant to turn quickly to avoid a collision. It was just enough to catch the Segway occupant off guard. But it all happened way too quickly to even be able to explain later what happened. One second Austin was at the end of the group struggling to catch up, and the next second he was grabbed and swallowed up by the darkness of the alley. The only evidence that he had actually been with the group was the Segway now lying on its side in the road.

There was no sound. Only darkness - made even deeper after being in the bright sunlight. Austin felt a stick in his arm, like a mosquito bite, that hurt for a second and then was forgotten.

Just as his eyes were adjusting to the darkness, he was shoved back out of the alley into the road next to his fallen Segway. It was as if nothing had really happened. One minute he was sailing along and then he wasn't. Then he was back picking up his Segway before anyone in his group even noticed his absence. With all that they had encountered, this occurrence seemed insignificant.

CHAPTER 17

Austin rejoined his group that had stopped for gelato – ice cream in Italy. The stinging in his arm had subsided, and pride kept him from mentioning his tumble into the dark alley since no one seemed to have even noticed. Thinking about it, Austin was relieved because he felt embarrassed about it, but, on the other hand, he also felt ignored. Oh well, heroes come and go.

When the groups met for lunch, Corrina separated herself from them to try to call Tuscon yet again and to go to the police station. She didn't make contact with anyone regarding Tuscon, and there was no new information from the police. Basically, they hadn't really searched for him. She was not able to convince them that he could be in danger. They still considered him gone of his own free will.

After lunch, while the students and chaperones rested in their rooms and packed for their evening two-and-a-half hour train ride to Venice, Corrina felt compelled to walk around the streets of Milan before leaving it to hopefully catch a glimpse of Tuscon, or discover a clue about his disappearance.

She didn't meet with success, but she wasn't

surprised. She had concluded that he didn't want to be found.

She decided that he had created the drama that had given him an excuse to abandon the group and run away from their carefully-made plans. Now she felt that he was determined to stay away from them and do his own thing. She never imagined what he might be capable of because until now there hadn't been a reason to speculate. Granted they knew little about him, but there had not been any reasons for questioning how he acted or what he said or did. How had they gotten to where they were right now? Why had he really left the group? Was he truly upset or was he just a good actor?

As she pondered all of these things, she felt worry for Tuscon turning to doubt and then anger while she walked from one street to another in front of bars and stores. She was slowly convincing herself that he had planned all along to disappear once he had arrived in Italy. He had used the convenience of their field trip to get what he wanted – easy entrance to a foreign country. Then she chastised herself for not checking each address, phone number, and detail for every student. What might she have found, especially about Tuscon?

What was further irritating to her was that losing a student on a field trip was a significant problem that would undoubtedly keep her from getting permission to take students on another trip.

That had other long-term effects since one of the major reasons students took her linguistic course was to go on field trips. Without field trips there would probably be less interest in taking her classes. Then there was also her teacher evaluation to consider, which would probably not be favorable considering the loss of a student.

As all this went through her head, she became angrier and began walking faster. It started on the plane. Well, actually, it had started in the airport. She began to wonder about what had happened that was suspicious. Then she realized that everything about Tuscon could be considered suspicious. And what about the warning she had received? Did that have anything to do with Tuscon? And now she was asking herself why she hadn't paid attention to the warning.

Even more important than the warning phone calls was what was happening right now that she didn't even know. Sometimes dangers lurk in quiet places. She was easily being followed because she was so deep in thought and unaware of her surroundings.

CHAPTER 18

At first, whoever was following Corrina stopped when she stopped and casually looked in windows as any shopper would. The difference was how close this person was getting without Corrina even noticing. Corrina just kept searching in crowds and bar windows for a face she recognized. She was therefore taken by surprise when a voice behind her said, "Corrina Morgan, don't turn around. Just keep walking and don't say anything. I'll do all the talking. You do the listening. And don't think you can outrun me. I guarantee that you can't. And since you don't carry a gun or a knife, I can also assure you that my weapons will hurt you, and I have no problem using them. In fact, I'm just looking for an excuse to use them. So you probably don't want to give me a reason to see how good I am at close range.

I could put this knife right in your back and keep on walking, and no one would see a thing until you collapsed on the sidewalk bleeding with a large hole in your back. And I would just keep walking while you might bleed to death. It seems to me that you've been given plenty of warnings, but you're not listening. Do you think you're too good to be threatened? That you're above the possibility of something serious happening to you? Do you think you're invincible? Are you surprised I know such a big word? You really are naïve. That's another big word. And here's another big thought. Would your students be able to survive the rest of this trip without you?

Now you're beginning to understand. I can tell because you're slowing down and I told you to keep walking. I can tell you're thinking, but I didn't tell you that you could slow down. So don't. Keep walking and facing forward because you don't want to know how I act when I get mad. That is just not a pretty sight. What I do like is that you're not talking. That's very good. There's nothing that you have to say that I want to hear. I do want something from you, though. It's a small thing really.

I want one of your students and I'll tell you which one. I have one picked out. You can keep the rest. I only want one. Nod your head if you're ready to hear which one. One nod will be sufficient. Are you ready to hear which student? I think you'll be surprised. But let me see your head nod first."

Corrina really had no option. You can see the dilemma she was in. Her choice was simple. Nod her head, which is what she did.

"Okay. I'm glad you're cooperating. Here goes. The student I want you to give me is Max. See? I knew you would be surprised. And just in case you think I'm kidding I want to assure you that I'm not. I'm deadly serious. And here's how we're going to play this game. I'm making the rules, so we're playing it the way I want to.

Today before you all get on the train to go to Venice, I want you to ask Max to do you a favor. Ask him to go back up to your room to check for something you can't find. After he gets on the elevator, you won't see him again. I'll take care of the rest. I'll contact his parents. You won't have to. Since his father is a board member, he will certainly take care of notifying your principal. You can count on that. I'd say soon after you arrive in Venice there will be another chaperone on their way from America to take over for you. After all, losing two students is just not acceptable. I'm sure you'll agree. And before you ever arrive back in the United States, you'll be jobless. Forget your career as a teacher. It's over. I would say that you'll also probably be arrested for aiding a kidnapper. I'm guessing they'll make that a felony and you'll go to prison. Now, let's review. You're going back to the hotel now to pack and gather your group in the lobby. Then you'll send Max up to your room, and your task will be finished. Just go on to Venice and see what happens next. Oh, you should just stop looking for Tuscon. You really won't see him again."

Up until now Corrina had remained quiet and just listened. Now she asked questions. "Why me? Why are you doing this? Why Max?"

The answer came quickly. "It's not you. Don't take it personally. You're just an innocent victim who happened to be a means to help me get what I want. You don't really know me, but I've been watching you for quite a while. Here's the catch.

You either cooperate with me or your parents back in D.C. won't be around to greet you when you get home."

CHAPTER 19

Many times Corrina had wondered what possessed a principal to give in to threats like Mark Rollins had done when twenty students were being kidnapped from his school three years ago. Now here she was facing the same dilemma. Maybe this was only an idle threat, but what if it's real? She thought she would test the theory by asking one final question as she turned to walk back toward the hotel.

"Do you even know my parents?"

After a nasty laugh, the answer was clear. "Do you mean Donna and John Morgan of 2012 Babcock Lane in Rockville, Maryland? Yes, I guess I do know them. Don't even think this is an idle threat. Now, go back to the hotel and do what you're supposed to do. I'll be waiting."

And so she did. She packed her clothes and belongings as she needed to. While she did so, she tried her parents' home phone number and both of their cell phones. No answers and no answering machine or voice mail kicked on.

She was left wondering, is this real? What if they really did already have her parents? What would happen if she called the police? Would they care?

How could she explain this? Could she call the police back home to check on her parents? How would she explain her concern? Just paranoia? The police in Italy would think she was crazy for sure. It seemed like they already did anyway. So should she just do what they told her to? But what if she really did lose another student? But what if they really did hurt her parents? She could never live with herself if that happened.

She decided that her only real option was going along with what they demanded to see what would happen. She could always get help later. This is known as the path of least resistance – just going along with something that you're not sure about rather than thinking about what else could be done. It's called taking the easy way out.

So she finished packing and left her room to meet the other chaperones and students in the lobby. When she saw Max she did as she had been told and asked him to go back up to her room to see if she forgot a book on the nightstand while she would wait for the rest of the students to arrive.

Max did as expected and got on the elevator. When the door closed, Corrina turned away. History repeats itself – if you don't do anything to stop it.

CHAPTER 20

Corrina had known it was too much to hope for that none of the students would ask where Max was. Corrina had decided that she could be vague with her response. It's amazing how gullible people can be. All she had to say was that he had forgotten something and she was waiting for him to get on one of the last cars of the train. That would satisfy their curiosity for now. Maybe by tomorrow morning they would forget to ask again. If what she had been told really happens tomorrow, then it wouldn't matter because she'd be replaced. Then they could all just wonder together where Max was, but what mattered to her would be that she and her parents would be safe. Right now that seemed to be the most important thing to Corrina. She wasn't being rational. Nor was she thinking like a teacher and a chaperone.

Through her irrational thoughts she had forgotten about Austin. Austin, who had saved the twenty kidnapped students when they were in middle school, was not to be forgotten or underestimated. Corrina might be able to count on the other students, and even the chaperones, not to worry much about Max being missing, but Austin was a different matter.

"Miss Morgan, where is Max?" Of course it was Austin asking.

Corrina responded as she had rehearsed in her mind. "He forgot something, so we'll get on the last car on the train to Venice. Now go ahead and get on the train with the others, and I'll wait for Max."

"Miss Morgan, I can wait with you so you won't be alone. I don't mind."

Corrina kept up the charade for now. "No, Austin, it's fine. We'll catch up to you all when we get to Venice. Go ahead now, get on the train with the others."

Austin knew when there was no reason to argue further, but he also knew when something wasn't right. This was definitely one of those times. He would just smile, walk away, and watch. What he saw surprised even Austin. From the window of his train car he saw Miss Morgan board the train on the next car – alone. There was no Max with her. He could see clearly that Miss Morgan was alone.

He continued to watch the door where Miss Morgan had entered, just assuming that he would see Max get in that train car before the train started moving. He didn't, and the train was now going.

With the two and a half-hour drive, Austin had time to sit and speculate what was happening. He could assume that Max had boarded the car ahead of Miss Morgan and he just hadn't seen him. He'd find everyone and start asking questions. But even Austin occasionally gets side-tracked, which occurred this time when he found Shawna.

"Hey, Shawna, can I sit here?"

Shawna gladly moved her bag to make room for Austin, smiling the entire time.

"So, Austin, what have you been up to? I haven't seen you all day."

Austin got right to the point. "I'm looking for Max. Have you seen him?"

Shawna, feeling mildly disappointed about the topic, still answered, "I heard Miss Morgan ask him to go up to her room to check to see if she'd forgotten her book. Then he went up on the elevator. I didn't see him after that, but he's probably on the train. He's pretty quiet. He might just be sitting and reading somewhere here on the train. Let's talk about something else besides Max. Wherever he is, he can take care of himself. What about you? Are you having a good time? It was great talking to you the other night at the restaurant. Maybe we can hang out together in Venice. Can you believe we'll be seeing the Basilica of Saint Mark and riding in a gondola in the Grand Canal? My mom said these are things most people only dream about, but we actually are getting to do them. What a fantastic trip this is! Miss Morgan is wonderful planning these trips for us kids. I wonder where she'll take us next time. I always wanted to see Paris and England. Where would you most want to go next year?"

At first, Austin's worries about Max were distracting him from Shawna's conversation. Now he was gradually becoming enthralled with Shawna and all that she had to say. Why not just enjoy the company of a cute freshman who obviously found him interesting and who wanted his attention. After all, he could worry about Max later. For now, he'd just relax where he was and spend two hours with Shawna, who had a smile that lit up even the dark train car.

CHAPTER 21

Corrina was feeling relieved that none of the students or chaperones had shown any great concern about Max. She felt like it was an indication of how everyone is caught up in their own lives and interests. She tried not to think that they didn't care. She wanted to believe they were just too busy to notice the world around them unless it made an impact on them.

Of course she didn't know that in another part of the train, Vanessa Walker was asking another chaperone, Don Barardi, if he knew if Max had gotten on the train with any of the other students because she thought she had seen him get back on the elevator when they were all meeting in the lobby to get ready to go to the train. Don replied that he had been running late himself getting down to the lobby because he had fallen asleep for too long and hadn't set an alarm. She said, "Well, I know what I saw, but apparently no one else noticed or cared."

Don responded as kindly as possible, "I don't know that no one cares. I just think it's difficult, especially in a foreign country, to keep everything together and get everywhere on time. I'm sure he's fine and with some of the other students. You'll see."

Always willing to share her unhappiness, and to express the final word on a topic, Vanessa said, "Well, I know what I've seen so far, and it's that it doesn't seem to matter if students disappear. Look at Tuscon. Here we are going about our business like everything was fine and all we have on our mind is going on the next tour or reaching the next destination. Don't you think more should have been done about him disappearing? Imagine if that had been one of the cheerleaders or football players. Then everyone would be frantic and looking everywhere. But because it's a student that no one knows anything about, it doesn't seem to matter."

Knowing there was no point to try to reason with her, Don decided in the dark to pretend like he was asleep. That may have been the coward's way out, but he really did feel too tired to listen to her or argue with her.

Other voices could be heard in the car. Listening closely, Max's name could be heard within several conversations. Either more people saw Max get on the elevator or they had just overheard the conversation between the two chaperones, Mrs. Walker and Mr. Barardi, and were speculating themselves about what had actually happened to Max. Were they really concerned or was it just a convenient topic of conversation to be had in the darkness on a boring train ride?

During his pretense of sleeping, Don could hear the conversations and felt guilty that he hadn't

been aware that something may have happened. Now

his thoughts were centered around Corrina. Why hadn't she communicated with him about Max? This is ridiculous.

How can two students be lost on a field trip? Where was Corrina anyway? He texted her, but didn't receive an immediate answer. With a sigh, Don thought, how can this trip be so complicated? What else could happen?

Well, as has been proven, just when you think things can't get worse, they do.

CHAPTER 22

Dr. Barry Pierce, the principal of National High School, received a phone call that left him extremely perplexed. With his busy summer between summer school, sports preparation, scheduling, and his own personal vacation to the beach, he had actually lost track of when the linguistic field trip was happening. It was so hard to keep track of everything. So, it came as a surprise to receive a phone call telling him that some people had one of his high school students and there was another one missing – "just in case you didn't know already" was what the caller had said. No, as a matter of fact, he didn't know. In fact, without looking at a list, he didn't even know what students or chaperones were on the trip. He assumed Corrina Morgan was there since she was the linguistic teacher. But where had he put that list? Surely he had filed it. Actually, no, it wasn't in the file.

It must still be in the pile on his desk of papers that still needed filed. The caller had given very little information, but said he would call back.

All he knew was there seemed to be two of his high school students unaccounted for on the trip to – where was that?

He really needed to find that paper, he thought before looking at the fall football schedule that the athletic director had given him yesterday. Meantime, textbooks arrived. A new student needed a schedule. An old student needed a transcript. The football coach stopped by to discuss the upcoming season. The student council advisor came to talk about plans for homecoming that was still two months away. The Superintendent, Mr. Harman Bernard, called with a question from a board member about something in the Student Handbook. Too many things to take care of. So, when the next phone call came in, he remembered that he still didn't know where the field trip was or who was on it.

CHAPTER 23

Dr. Pierce was just ready to leave his office after his very busy day. It's hard to imagine how an entire day in the summer without teachers and students could be so exhausting. Now he was looking forward to a cool drink of sun-brewed iced tea on his patio while he grilled some juicy hamburgers for dinner. It was already past four o'clock and he had his briefcase in his hand when the phone rang. He had a half-hour drive to the suburbs ahead of him and he momentarily considered not answering the phone.

Who could be calling so late on a summer day, he thought as he answered with his typical greeting, "National High School, a great place to learn. This is Barry Pierce." As he automatically responded, his brain played back the earlier phone call this morning about the missing students on the field trip.

So it wasn't a complete surprise to hear that same voice. He also had a second for a part of his brain to wish he had followed up with finding the paper that listed the students and destinations of the linguistics field trip. But he hadn't, and so he was at the mercy of whatever the caller told him.

"Hello, Dr. Pierce. I'm sure you've been

expecting my call. In case you're wondering, Tuscon is quite an asset and hasn't been located. Now about your boy, Max. Max Sterling. You remember him, right? That name should sound familiar to you. John Sterling? He's still on the Board of Education, right? Sure he is. I've checked. Well, Max happens to be his little boy. Although he's grown up since he was last kidnapped. Imagine what's in his mind being kidnapped twice in his life. I wonder what his daddy's going to say. I bet he's not going to be real happy with you. The last principal at your middle school lost his job over that other kidnapping. It was all over national news. How much do you like your job, Dr. Pierce?"

Thoughts of drinking iced tea and sitting on his patio were now gone as he sat down at his desk and dropped his briefcase on the floor.

"Barry Pierce, are you there? Do I have your attention now? What do you have to say? Do you like your job?"

Dr. Pierce was rarely speechless and even more rarely taken by surprise. Although quiet and seemingly disorganized, he was effective at his job and was usually on top of everything that was happening. But he had never been faced with something like this.

He took a deep breath before responding, "Whether I like my job or not is not the concern here. What is the concern is that you are admitting to kidnapping at least one student, and possibly two. Kidnapping is a felony and you are admitting to it. You'd better have a good lawyer because when you're caught, you're going to need one."

Now anger was evident in the caller's voice as he replied, "You're missing the point, Dr. Pierce. Whether I go to prison or not won't help to find Tuscon or Max alive. They may never be found. Now you listen to me very carefully. Playing tough guy with me is not helping Max right now. He's still alive and he's right here. Would you like to talk to him? I'm sure he'd love to talk to his principal. Here's Max."

Sounds of the phone being passed to another person could be heard, and then a voice saying, "Dr. Pierce, I'm sorry. I thought I was just helping Miss Morgan. I didn't know it was a trick."

Immediately there were sounds of the phone being grabbed back, and then, "Just in case you needed proof. Well, there it is. We have Max and here's what you, Dr. Pierce, need to do."

Still not completely intimidated by the caller claiming to have Max, Dr. Pierce again attempted his own take-charge attitude that worked with students and parents, by interrupting, "No. Let me tell you what you need to do. Max is a minor. A child in the eyes of the law. I am hanging up and calling the police. This time we'll get them involved at the beginning of your threats. You're not going to get away with kidnapping like you did last time."

"First, Dr. Pierce, I can assure you that I had nothing to do with the last kidnapping in your district. I know about it because it was all over the news. Secondly, as I recall, no one got away with that kidnapping, as you're saying. They all went to prison, but I can tell you, that won't happen to me. I'm going to hang up now to give you time to think about whether you should get the police involved."

Then, almost as an after-thought, the caller said, "Remember, I've got Max and you've got a job for now. If you don't handle this whole thing the right way, you'll probably not have a job and Max won't see America again. Right now I'm going to go see how afraid Max is of the dark. He's fifteen. He should be okay. But, the rat's smell fear. Remember that when you're making your decisions."

And then there was only silence on the phone line.

CHAPTER 24

Dr. Pierce sat in his office for a long time staring and thinking. His cell phone began to ring. As he expected, it was his wife. He wondered, as he answered, if she would be a good person to confide in. He needed to discuss this with someone, but he wasn't sure yet if she might be the one who could listen and understand his dilemma. Right now she just wondered how soon he was coming home and would he be able to stop to buy some lettuce for a salad on his way to the house. He agreed to buy the lettuce and said he'd be there in about forty-five minutes. That meant he needed to leave now.

Call the police. Don't call the police. Would it hurt to wait until after his dinner and a conversation with his wife to decide what to do? He couldn't see that any harm could come from waiting. After all, it was night time in Italy, so probably everyone was asleep. He would leave the office now, stop for lettuce, grill hamburgers, and talk to his wife later tonight to get her opinion. She was a nurse, not an educator, but she had strong opinions and a lot of intelligence to back up what she thought about most topics. She didn't have a lot of knowledge about sports, so that was one topic they didn't discuss, but he felt certain that she'd have some intelligent thoughts about kidnappers taking high school students while they were on a trip to Italy.

While Dr. Pierce was debating about whether to get law enforcement in the United States involved, in another part of the world Miss Morgan was gathering her belongings to exit the train in Venice without any thoughts of calling the police. She had tried that before and it hadn't helped to try to get them involved about finding Tuscon. This was also a different situation. She didn't want her parents harmed, so she was just going to keep doing her duties as a chaperone and pretend like this field trip was like any other one that she had taken with students. After all, she wasn't involved with the kidnapping in their district three years ago. That was someone else's mistake and she just wasn't going to let that influence what she did on this trip. It didn't seem like anyone else cared either, or so she thought, but she couldn't hear the questions and rumors spreading about her.

As other chaperones and students disembarked from the train in Venice and got their first glimpse at the beautiful canals by night, their thoughts and discussions were not just on the beauty before them, but on the absence of two of their peers.

Some of the girls were especially beginning to feel stress as word spread about what some had seen in the lobby of the hotel when Miss Morgan sent Max up the elevator and then left without him. And what about Tuscon? She hadn't even acted concerned as they all went about their plans like nothing was wrong.

Now, here was Miss Morgan with her list checking off students as they got off the train and just skipping over Tuscon and Max's names like they no longer existed. Besides stress, there was also growing fear. Who was next and would Miss Morgan care?

As students generally do, even young adults as these students were, when things don't seem right, they began calling each other's cell phones. Sounds of cell phones ringing and texts being received could be heard throughout the group as they gathered to catch the bus to their hotel rooms in the middle of the night. They could see Mr. Barardi and Mr. Sutton trying to talk to Miss Morgan, but she just kept looking at her lists and checking off names. Students began to whisper among themselves and also to Miss Tichnell and even to Mrs. Walker. Like everyone else, they had no answers, but that didn't stop Mrs. Walker from voicing her opinion to anyone who would listen and to even those who didn't care to listen.

"I think there's definitely something wrong when two students just disappear. Can you imagine? If they didn't show up at school for a day, we'd be calling their parents. But here we are in a strange country and they're nowhere to be found, and we just go about our business like nothing's wrong. This is the strangest thing I've ever seen, and we're just going to our next location in the middle of the night and there are kids missing! Has anyone even called their parents? You know, we all have their phone numbers. I think I'll just do that myself. Max's parents need to know their son won't be coming home ever again. As soon as I'm in my room, I'm going to make that call."

And that's how it happened that Dr. Pierce's hamburgers on the grill got burned to a crisp and his world started to change.

CHAPTER 25

Dr. Barry Pierce was finally unwinding from his day at the high school with his cool drink of iced tea in one hand and the spatula in the other standing over the grill. Yes, it was later than he had planned, but at least the temperature had dropped slightly and there was a breeze on his patio in his back yard. It's all going to be okay, he thought. Over dinner he would talk to his wife and get some of her wisdom about how to handle the situation.

The tension in his neck and shoulders was easing and the drink was helping to get rid of his headache when his cell phone rang. He put down the drink and the spatula on the table and reached for his phone as he looked at caller I.D. It was never good when a board member called him. In this case, it was definitely not good that it was John Sterling. Although they had golfed together a few times, Barry had a moment to think, I bet this isn't about getting together for a golf outing, before answering, "This is Barry Pierce."

Without an introduction, John Sterling was yelling when he said, "Dr. Pierce, where is my son? Have you called the police? What did Miss Morgan tell you? I had to hear this from Vanessa Walker."

Pausing only for a second, Mr. Sterling continued, "Why haven't you called me? Superintendent Bernard hasn't informed me. Does he even know?"

Taking a deep breath, Dr. Pierce had time to reflect and think, good ol' Mrs. Walker. Of course, she would get involved. Interfering is what she does best, before attempting to answer Mr. Sterling's questions. Not knowing where to start, he simply and honestly began.

"Mr. Sterling, I don't know where Max is. Quite frankly, I'm not even sure what city they're in. I know they're in Italy somewhere." He thought quickly before continuing, do I tell him about the call from the kidnappers? Withholding information could cause him grief later. However, being honest now would show that he hadn't done anything when he first found out that Max was kidnapped. In that moment, Barry Pierce made the decision to do the right thing and be totally honest. The outcome of telling the truth would later be determined.

"Mr. Sterling, I received a phone call from Max's possible kidnappers this afternoon. Because it is night time in Italy, I didn't know what could be done." He left out the part about needing a cool drink and a hamburger.

Max's father and board member, John Sterling, was not as calm this time as he had been the first time his son had been kidnapped. Obviously having your only child kidnapped twice in three years and hearing about it from a disgruntled employee had taken its immediate toll on Mr. Sterling.

Mr. Sterling's answer was simple, "I'll call the police and you call the superintendent. I'll be calling you back in a few minutes." So Barry Pierce didn't get a chance to tell him that they shouldn't be calling the police before Max's father hung up.

And so the nightmare began, or continued, depending on if you were one of the parents or students involved in the previous kidnapping in this district three years ago. How could this happen twice?

CHAPTER 26

Corrina Morgan felt like she had been on a roller coaster without being able to get off. She was so relieved to be in her hotel room alone with the door closed. Although it would only be for a few hours, she just wanted to crawl into bed and pull the covers over her head, but that wasn't going to happen. She needed to think. Although she had turned the sound off on her phone, she had also turned it over to keep from seeing it light up with voice mail and text messages. She didn't want to answer to anyone right now. They were all distracting her from what she needed to do.

She started by calling her sister. Although it was late evening in the United States, she knew her sister would still be awake and putting kids to bed. She also knew that her sister talked to their parents every day and would know if anything was wrong with them. After a brief chat about kids and Corrina's trip so far, with Corrina leaving out much of it, Corrina asked how their mom and dad were.

She was met with her current fear from what her sister said, "I don't know today. This afternoon when I called, there was no answer. Mom had talked about going to visit Aunt Grace and Uncle Walter sometime soon, but I don't know if she did. And Dad might have been outside."

Pausing to say something to one of her children, Corrina's sister continued, "You know how Dad likes to work in the yard. So I don't really know why I didn't get an answer when I called. I'll try again tomorrow" before ending the call.

Hanging up quickly, Corrina knew it was useless for her to lecture her sister about how it was her responsibility with Corrina out of the country to check on their parents. She also knew already that tomorrow might be too late. Who could she trust? She wished she knew someone she could talk to.

Exhaustion took over and so Corrina didn't realize that she received a phone call that went to voice mail until morning. While everyone else did not rest peacefully, Corrina slept for several hours before looking at her phone. A text message from the kidnapper was brief, "I told you not to call the police." Her heart began to race and she felt sick. Even while she heard knocking on her hotel room door, she ignored it and dialed her parents' phone number in the United States. There was no answer again. She knew deep inside of her that the kidnappers had been serious, but she hadn't been the one who called the police. Whoever had made that phone call had started a chain of events that could now not be stopped.

But there wasn't time to think about it now. She had to go downstairs and keep up the charade.

CHAPTER 27

While the students and chaperones were gathering in the lobby for their excursion that would take them to see the Bridge of Sighs on the Rio di Palazzo and glide in a gondola along the Grand Canal, Corrina pretended that everything was normal. She ignored their questions, brushed past the other chaperones, and encouraged them all to come eat breakfast in the dining room of the hotel before embarking on a day's adventure in the beautiful city of Venice, Italy. Breakfast in Italy is usually light, but all the chaperones and students were extremely hungry from the late-night adventure, which was perfect since a special cake seemed to have been delivered for this group to eat along with their cappuccino and tea. No explanation was given except for a note delivered with the cake that read, *For National High School's Linguistic Club. Eat hearty.*

As odd as this was, it was funny how no one questioned where the cake had come from, but there it was just for them. In Italy, breakfast wasn't a big deal, so being able to order bacon and eggs or a stack of pancakes was out of the question. This cake was what was available and they were all too hungry to ask questions.

In addition, they had learned from Miss Morgan not to appear ungrateful in restaurants in Italy because it would seem rude. So they all ate cake. Lots of cake, which was called dolce o frutta, or dessert with fruit. While eating, they all glanced at Miss Morgan at various times, but she didn't make eye contact. She just seemed to stare. That was it. She was just eating and staring and ignoring any discussions around her even when Mr. Barardi and Mr. Sutton talked to her directly. It was like she didn't hear them. Like there wasn't anything important to discuss, when they all knew there was something very frightening going on that she seemed to be ignoring. It was definitely a perfect example of the saying, "ignoring the elephant in the room." Even while chewing, many in the room felt like screaming, "Where's Max? Did you hear from Tuscon?" But the elephant went on being ignored. And to an outsider, it all seemed like a perfect little American group of teenagers and adults ready to embark on an exciting day in Venice, except that gradually one by one they all began to clutch their stomachs and turn pale.

All but Melanie. Melanie was the only one continuing to sit there and smile. Austin was perceptive enough to see that. He looked around and could tell immediately that something was very wrong. Even the chaperones were desperately searching with their eyes for a sign saying *toilette* that meant there were restrooms close by, but Melanie was smiling.

Brianna, despite her own aching stomach, also saw Melanie smiling. Austin's eyes met Brianna's and without saying anything there was an understanding that Melanie not only had not eaten the cake, but seemed pleased that everyone was sick.

It felt like a confirmation of what Brianna had guessed all along – there was something sinister beneath the smiling surface of Melanie Swiger. Although Brianna had not ever had that conversation with Austin to acknowledge him saving her from the fall when Melanie had pushed her, she knew Austin remembered. His look right now said it all.

As Melanie quietly got up from the table while answering her cell phone, Brianna followed her to the hall while discreetly staying behind her. With Melanie engaged in the phone conversation, she was unaware that Brianna was standing behind a column listening. One side of the conversation was all that Brianna needed to hear to know that Melanie was involved and it was not a coincidence that they were all sick. From where Brianna stood, Melanie could clearly be heard saying, "Yes, they're all ready to throw up." After a pause, Melanie's next words left Brianna feeling shocked and sick at the same time, which caused her to not see the shadow behind her. Before Brianna could hear more, her world went dark.

When Brianna woke up, Miss Morgan was kneeling beside her holding ice on the bump on her head and talking softly to her, telling her it was all going to be fine. Brianna couldn't remember where she was for a few seconds, but then it came to her as she turned sideways on the floor and vomited. They were all sick and Brianna remembered suddenly that Melanie knew why. While trying to keep from gagging more, she tried to tell Miss Morgan all about who Melanie was talking to on the phone, but all Miss Morgan did was pat her arm and say, "You're going to be fine," even while Miss Morgan herself was pale and looked nauseated.

What was going on here? Even Austin, who came and knelt beside Brianna, seemed to be hushing her with silent signals from his eyes, telling her to not talk about it. Brianna thought, are they all crazy, as she vomited again.

All the other students and chaperones were moaning as they left the restaurant. They were all in such pain that most didn't even notice Brianna on the floor still behind the column. Melanie was long gone as if she were just part of the group. But, Austin knew, and he offered his help. "Miss Morgan, since you're obviously not feeling well either, how about I'll help you and Brianna up to your rooms?"

Corrina managed to shake her head as she replied, "No," and motioned them to leave her alone. Not waiting to offer a second time, Austin helped Brianna to her feet, leaving the mess and Miss Morgan on the floor in the hallway. As he walked with his arm around Brianna's shoulders through the lobby, he said to the man at the front desk, "Lei sta male" in Italian, which meant 'She is sick' and pointed toward the hall from where they had come. Austin hoped the man understood his mediocre Italian as he walked Brianna toward the elevator to take her to her room.

He asked her room number as they entered the elevator, but again motioned for her to be quiet as she started to explain again what she had heard. Although alone in the elevator, he pointed upward toward a camera in the corner that he felt certain also had a listening device. He couldn't imagine that it only captured visual images.

CHAPTER 28

As sick as Brianna felt, she wanted to drag Austin down the hall to hurry and tell him what she overheard. However, Austin also could hardly move without his head swimming and his stomach gurgling, and so they moved delicately. But they didn't make it to Brianna's room. It all happened in one motion as someone stepped out of a room, grabbed Austin from behind, and pulled him into one of the rooms before Brianna could even think what was happening.

One second she and Austin were helping each other down the hall and, in the next instant, Brianna was alone in the hallway with the only sound being a slamming door. Her eyes were blurring and she couldn't tell which room it was because it happened so fast, but she knew she needed to get to her room right now before she vomited in the hallway. There was not time now, but she would come right back.

Within a few minutes in her room, Brianna felt temporarily relieved and realized that concerns over her own comfort could be costing Austin his life. She went back out into the hall and felt completely confused about what room Austin had been drug into.

Her only choice was to start pounding on

doors. Some rooms didn't seem to have occupants. Maybe people were just afraid to answer the door to what probably seemed like a crazy American teenage girl asking for help. She knew it had happened somewhere right around here, and so she started yelling Austin's name. A few strangers opened their doors and just shook their heads. Jason, another student on their trip, and Austin's roommate, came to his door and started to ask what was wrong, but then held up his hand as if to say, I've got to go, and then he ran to the door of his bathroom. That didn't help Brianna. What was this mysterious illness that had taken over their group, she wondered as she moved on and continued to yell Austin's name. Even as she searched, she remembered Melanie telling someone on the phone that everyone was sick.

As Brianna turned from one door to another, she felt strongly that the idea of people just disappearing was unbelievable, but she had seen it with her own eyes. She had felt Austin beside her and then he was gone. He had saved her one time and then even today had helped her, but now here she was feeling completely helpless to help him. She realized that the obvious thing to do was to call Miss Morgan. She would know what to do. While continuing her search in the hallway, she tried Miss Morgan's number on her cell phone, but all she accomplished was leaving the message, "Miss Morgan, this is Brianna. Austin has disappeared. I need your help. Please call me."

Unknown to Brianna, Miss Morgan listened to the message immediately, and thought, not again. This can't be happening. But now Corrina felt relief, which was a strange feeling considering the circumstances.

If anyone saw Corrina Morgan at this moment, they would wonder at the broad smile on her face, as her thoughts became clearer. Now she said to herself, everything is going to be just fine. It's all falling into place. All of our lives are about to change.

Brianna had different thoughts, though. She had heard Melanie speaking to the probable kidnappers, and what she had heard made her desperate to talk to Miss Morgan. Not only was Austin in great danger, but Max may have already lost his life at the hands of the kidnappers. Since she couldn't reach Miss Morgan, she would try Mr. Barardi and Mr. Sutton. Hopefully they weren't too sick to meet with her. Similar to previous thoughts that Corrina Morgan had experienced, Brianna felt like she was the only one concerned about any of this. She felt like she was having a bad dream, actually a nightmare, that no one else was having and she was out there all alone while it seemed that no one else was worried. Although it may seem that everyone on her trip with her was uncaring about this strange situation, she had no way of knowing what was happening right here in the city of Venice, but maybe even more importantly, what was happening in another part of the world.

CHAPTER 29

Corrina's intuition had warned her last spring that something wasn't right. She had sensed that feeling before they ever left the United States. Now she assumed that what was happening with missing students was the bad thing she had dreaded from her intuition. She was wrong thinking this was it. She never imagined what was yet to come.

As directed, Dr. Barry Pierce had called the superintendent. That led to an unpleasant conversation in the morning that included a stressful review of the previous kidnapping event from three years ago that had led to the close monitoring of field trips. Now look where they are! Someone should have been watching more closely to prevent this kind of tragedy again. "Yes." The superintendent reminded Dr. Pierce, "This is a tragedy. Losing children is our biggest fear. And now you're trying to explain how your teacher managed to lose not one, but two students! As superintendent I can't imagine anything worse."

Maybe if people would just quit thinking that the worst had happened, the world would possibly return to normal again. Even the superintendent couldn't imagine worse, but he didn't know how desperate people can be when they want revenge.

Dr. Pierce sat thinking in his office. He personally saw little connection to the kidnapping three years ago. Why had the superintendent brought up the past? We didn't need that kind of attention brought to the school district again. That was all in the past, and the less that it was remembered, the better off they all were. That had been the mistake by another principal and his wife. Mark Rollins had lost his job as the middle school principal, and his wife, Liz Rollins, had spent some time in prison. They were out of the picture and there was no reason to even discuss them. Barry felt confident that he would never do something as irresponsible as sending twenty students on a bus with a kidnapper. But, did he ever think he would allow twelve students and five chaperones to go on a trip that could end with a tragedy like they were now experiencing? Not likely. He wasn't typically a risk-taker. He didn't involve himself with anything questionable. He and his wife were both very careful people. But what if their son happened to be missing? He knew deep inside that all of his rational thinking might be lost.

For a brief second he almost understood John Sterling's frustration, but then thought further – we need to stay calm and reasonable to get these students back. While feeling helpless, he decided that there was one productive action he could take. Sitting down at his desk, he looked up the phone number of Mark Rollins.

Maybe to prevent something more catastrophic

he should talk to the one person who had lived through it and could maybe give some advice from his own experience.

Surprisingly, Mark Rollins answered his home phone almost immediately. "Mark, this is Barry Pierce – the principal at National High School. How are you?"

Barry could detect a brief hesitancy and then a friendly greeting. "Barry. It's been a while. I'm doing okay. How are things going in the education world?" Although three years had separated their last conversation until now, education has its own comradery and collegiality that doesn't go away. It's like a bond that exists through time because of having been through experiences together. It's why class reunions still exist. The bond of living through common occurrences together and getting to the other side isn't easily broken. After all the principal meetings they had sat through together, Barry Pierce was the only person that Mark Rollins had confided in and shared his regrets when he had lost his job as the middle school principal. Now Barry was seeking Mark's help.

Barry responded, "Well, as you can imagine, life is never dull in education. What are you doing without that kind of stress?"

Mark laughed, "I'm selling insurance. Now isn't that a strange turn of events? There are actually people out there who'll buy insurance from me to pay for the bad things that could happen in their lives."

Mark continued, "I guess who better to warn them about those unexpected twists and turns that life can throw at you than me. Right? We sure don't know from one day to the next what might come at us. Who knew that one strange phone call could change a life and wipe out a career? No classes we took to be a principal ever prepared me for that one."

Seizing the opportunity, Barry began his story about the way his life had changed since a phone call yesterday. Mark patiently listened and then asked, "What can I do to help?" Now that's a true friend and someone you want on your side when the chips are down. Someone who's been through it, learned something from it, and offers to do whatever he can to help.

Barry's answer to Mark's question was simple. "You tell me. What do you think I should do?"

CHAPTER 30

Max's father, John Sterling, received a simple ransom note through a text on his cell phone that said, "We've got Max. It will cost you to see him alive." Then nothing. He sprang into action immediately. This time he was not going to sit idly by and wait for something to happen. He quickly made plane reservations for his wife and himself. They were going to go to Italy and take care of this and get their son back. Money was not the issue. Making people understand that doing the right thing would keep Max safe until he was returned to them was what would make a difference, and he felt that he was the one to do that. This was not going to be tolerated again while he was on the Board of Education. One kidnapping experience was more than enough. Twice was more than he could stand as a father and board member. He felt anger surfacing within his mind again. Adrenaline had started rushing immediately when he had received the phone call from Vanessa Walker. Now he felt uncontrollable rage. "That's it," he said to his wife as they both hurriedly threw clothes into suitcases. "I'm calling the FBI."

Now, interestingly enough, the FBI – Federal Bureau of Investigation – is just that. It's federal.

That means the United States inside of its borders. Once citizens of the United States leave the jurisdiction of their country, their problems become someone else's concerns. Or not. Once again, as Corrina Morgan had found out, it just depends on whether someone you talk to decides your concerns are worth worrying about. As you can imagine, John Sterling was not happy or satisfied with this information. In other words, he would be at the mercy of European government agencies to help him unless he could get someone in the FBI to make a connection, a real human intervention, to someone in Europe who would care.

As luck would have it, he was connected to someone who just happened to care and knew who to call in Europe. There are usually scores to even and favors to pay back in the life of someone whose job it is to make things right in the world. He had found that person, and connections would be made, and discreet phone calls would be placed. "You and your wife just get on that plane. The rest will be taken care of. Let us do our job."

That person didn't know John Sterling very well. John wasn't the kind of person to let someone just do his job.

CHAPTER 31

Brianna's search in the hallway for Austin had led to nothing but more worry. Miss Morgan had not returned her phone call, and Mr. Barardi and Mr. Sutton weren't answering her texts. She felt close to tears, but she knew that crying was not going to help her find Austin. She also knew that Austin hadn't given up when students were kidnapped three years ago when his persistence had saved all the students, and she wouldn't give up on Austin now. There had to be someone who could help her.

It occurred to Brianna that she wasn't seeing anyone she knew in the hallways. Maybe everyone was so sick they couldn't come out of their rooms. She decided that surely someone at the hotel's front desk would know where everyone was. She pushed the button and waited for the elevator to come, not expecting any solution to her problem when the door opened. At first she couldn't believe what she was seeing. Her stress must be making her delusional, she thought, right before processing the scene in front of her. There stood Austin holding hands with Shawna like they had been together forever.

Brianna found her voice and spoke quickly and

loudly, "Austin, what are you doing?"

Shawna seemed to be more than happy to answer Brianna's question. "What's it look like he's doing? He's with me."

Brianna's reply was directed to Austin while ignoring Shawna. "Austin, you disappeared. I've been looking for you the entire time since you were pulled into that room. Where did you go? What have you been doing?"

Brianna's voice was rising to a high pitch as the elevator doors began to close. "No! I'm not losing you again. Wherever you're going, I'm going with you." She entered the elevator just in time before the doors snapped shut, but Shawna's hissed words could clearly be heard, "Brianna, I don't know what your problem is, but Austin is with me. I saw him in the hallway a few minutes ago and asked him to spend the day with me here in Venice. We're on our way to the lobby to meet with the group to go on our tour. He said he had been sick, but he looks fine now. Austin, tell her you're with me. I don't know anything about him disappearing. I think you're just jealous because you want Austin. Well, now he's mine."

Brianna, still sure of what she had seen happen in the hallway, said, "Austin, tell her. Tell her what happened to us this morning."

By now the elevator doors were opening into the lobby as Austin leaned toward Brianna while stepping out. He whispered for only Brianna to hear, "I'll text you later." Then he was off to join the large group by the front door, leaving Brianna still confused.

Brianna really had no choice at that moment,

so she stood with the others, looking around to see if everyone looked recovered from their stomach illness. Then she received a text from Austin. She looked up and met his eyes briefly through the crowd before reading what he had sent her. "They let me go. I couldn't help them, so I was of no use to them. They seem to always know where I am. Watch out for Melanie."

Brianna was left with many unanswered questions. Who had taken Austin? What had they wanted? How was Melanie involved? What could Melanie do to hurt her? She knew she needed to be brief, and texted back to Austin, "Who do you mean by *they*?" Austin's answer was simple, but not very informative, "A man and a woman."

But an agenda was made for a reason, and so the trip went on as planned. To Brianna it felt like a never-ending nightmare. Many thoughts were going through her head. How calm everyone was. What is wrong with them? They act like nothing has happened. And here comes Miss Morgan with her clipboard, checking off people again. The stomach problems all seemed gone. We're back to only two students missing. Only two students missing! Am I the only sane person here?

CHAPTER 32

The city of Venice in Italy looks now like it did in the 13th century. The Grand Canal still divides Venice into two parts with palaces lining the sides right at the edges of the water. Instead of streets, there are waterways. The best way to see the palaces of Venice is to ride in a gondola, which is a long narrow flat-bottomed boat, through the Grand Canal. Although an expensive trip, it would be a shame for visitors to be in Venice and not ride in a gondola. So, despite all that was happening, the group divided into gondolas for their adventure that would offer memories for a lifetime, in more ways than one.

Brianna saw Austin get into a gondola with Shawna. While slightly disappointed, she settled into a gondola with Jessica and Celeste. From where Brianna was sitting, she glanced around to see where Melanie was, and when she saw her in the same gondola that she was in, she was relieved that two of the chaperones, Mr. Barardi and Mr. Sutton, were in this same gondola. She knew there wasn't much that Melanie could get away with while she was so close to two of their chaperones.

At least that's what Brianna believed, but she

didn't think about all that could still be accomplished through cell phones even from a gondola in the Grand Canal of Venice. So while they floated under bridges and past palaces, churches, and museums, Melanie kept up a running dialogue with someone through texting. Brianna thought that it would be quite interesting to know who was on the other end.

That was yet to become obvious when they reached their final destination on today's tour, which would end at the Piazza San Marco and the Doges' Palace. High above the Piazza San Marco is the bell tower with a belfry where Galileo had tried out his telescope back in the 16th century, according to what their tour guide was telling them.

Melanie barely raised her head from her texting to look at the sights as they floated down the Grand Canal. Brianna attempted to concentrate on all that the tour guide in the gondola was telling them, but her mind kept wandering and imagining what Melanie was involved in. Brianna still felt disappointed in Miss Morgan's lack of concern from the message she had left on Miss Morgan's voice mail. Brianna had not gotten to share with anyone what she had overheard Melanie say that morning in the hotel. It seemed so long ago, but here they all were, recovered from their stomach problems and all in the same day touring Venice like everything was normal. Other people surely must know there was evil lurking in the shadows waiting to come out. It was only a matter of time.

As Brianna's mind wandered from what the tour guide was saying, her eyes fell again on Melanie, who was now staring in her direction. Brianna's mind flashed once again to her near fatal fall at the high school as she once more regretted not reporting that Melanie had pushed her. Even now, as she sat in a gondola in Venice, she wished she would have told someone, or even acknowledged Austin saving her. She now realized the importance of needing to report it because it would be additional evidence against Melanie, the perfect smiling cheerleader, when she was caught in whatever she was involved in on this trip. But no one would believe her now, thought Brianna, and she knew that wishing she had done something different in the past wouldn't change what was happening now – two students missing and Melanie still smiling.

CHAPTER 33

The gondola ride had provided a spectacular view of the Piazza San Marco even before they arrived. Parts of it led directly to the Adriatic Sea. This area felt like a city itself with a history of its own. While the architecture made it seem elegant beyond words, there was a somber look to the buildings that made the idea of being there after dark seem a little frightening. It was like the shadows even in the bright sunlight were ominous and foreboding. Despite the intense heat in the air and radiating from the bricks and stone of the buildings, Brianna shivered as she looked around her to locate Melanie. She had lost track of her as they had emerged from the gondolas.

Now she searched the crowd for any sign of Melanie or Austin, or even Shawna, but as she looked around, the only person she recognized from their school was Raianna. She hadn't realized that she had become separated from their group, and Raianna was too far ahead of her in the crowd to call out her name. She would have to enter the building alone until she saw someone that she recognized. She thought it was one thing to roam hotel halls by herself, but to enter and explore a temple and museum that were both centuries old, alone without anyone she knew, didn't appeal to her. She considered waiting outside, but she knew that wouldn't help her get with the rest of her group because all of these buildings were connected and led from one to the other.

If she stayed where she was, she would possibly not find the other students from the high school until they all joined together again back at the hotel tonight or tomorrow morning. She needed to keep moving with the crowd. She had no choice. If Brianna had not been so focused on whether to enter the building alone or not, she might have seen someone watching her from the shadows. As she entered the San Marco, the person in the shadow became visible and disappeared into the crowd behind Brianna.

Four large bronze horses from the year 1250 were standing within the temple along with marble statues that Brianna passed as she made her way deeper into the temple through the atrium and gallery past arches and columns that represented older times in history. There were tombs and altars and crypts and more statues. While beautiful works of art and tapestries vaguely penetrated her subconscious, Brianna became more determined to find Miss Morgan to tell her what she had overheard Melanie saying to someone on the phone during breakfast, which seemed so long ago – not just this morning. The overall solemn feeling that she sensed from being here made telling someone her concerns seem even more urgent.

She was blending with the crowd as it flowed from where she had started in the Piazza San Marco to what was called the Palace of the Doges, which had been built with towers to defend the castle from enemy attacks from the sea. Through a corridor and then into a hall, they were told that a passage from there would lead to the Bridge of Sighs and from there to the prisons. A stairway called the Golden Staircase had been used for official ceremonies. They were shown two doors that opened off the staircase with one leading to an apartment where the doge had lived when he was the head of the church and the political leader.

A drawing room located at the top of the stairs contained more works of art. Brianna heard the tour guide ahead of her point out a secret passageway beside a throne. The tour guide ended most of the explanations with the word, "Guardare (look at)."

There were other stairways and corridors that led to cells where prisoners had been kept. They were shown one cell labelled with a Roman numeral VII that was still covered completely by wooden boards with a wooden pallet that would have probably been a bed with a small wooden shelf on the wall. It was a frightening, deserted looking place that would certainly have led a prisoner to feel isolated. Although there was bright sunshine outside of this building, here there was only darkness lit with dull light that left most of the room in darkness. What was in the corners could only be imagined, but not seen.

CHAPTER 34

As fascinating as this tour was, Brianna slipped away and followed the corridor back to where she thought she had joined this group, but after being shown many hallways and staircases, she soon became disoriented and totally confused. At each intersection, she debated whether to turn left or right and tried once again to use her cell phone, which so far had picked up sporadic service within this stone fortress. Once again, she couldn't get a signal and was still separated from anyone else from the high school.

Just as she was deciding whether or not to give up and find a way to get back out to the daylight, she saw a familiar face at the end of the corridor she was in now. At least the back of the person's head looked like Miss Morgan walking beside Mrs. Walker. She felt like running to catch them, but knew not to do that in a museum containing fragile objects. Miss Morgan had lectured them before they made the trip about appropriate public behavior. Brianna instead decided to just keep watching them and hope that she wouldn't lose sight of them. She was doing well, and even gaining on them when they abruptly turned right. She hurried to where they had turned, and was relieved to see them ahead when she turned into the same passageway where they were, and knew she would be able to close the distance between them.

Just then, a group of loud tourists stepped out in front of her and blocked her view. By the time they stopped to look at their map, and Brianna could get around them, she had lost sight of Miss Morgan and Mrs. Walker. Brianna reminded herself that she was a resourceful person. She knew she hadn't gotten this far in her life by being a quitter, and she wouldn't give up now. She felt grateful that she hadn't seen Melanie and she knew that Miss Morgan and probably the other chaperones had to be somewhere in this building. She had just seen two of them. The rest couldn't be far away. She would just keep going.

Finally, there was Miss Morgan just ahead. This time Brianna moved quickly and finally got close enough to call her name. "Miss Morgan, wait. I need to talk with you. Miss Morgan!"

She must have gotten Miss Morgan's attention because Brianna saw her slow down and glance behind her. For the first time, Brianna noticed a difference in Miss Morgan. There was a look of tiredness and stress on her face. She looked haggard and unhappy. This was not the typical demeanor of Miss Morgan. Usually she was vivacious and energetic, but not now.

For a second, Brianna was reluctant to tell her what she had heard Melanie say this morning. However, that hesitancy passed, and Brianna started immediately when she caught up with the two chaperones. In her haste, Brianna failed to notice Miss Morgan shaking her head and holding up her hands as if to stop Brianna from saying too much, but Brianna was so anxious to share what she knew that she just forged ahead. Brianna also didn't see the person who had been closely following her stop only a few feet away as if inspecting closely a painting on an easel.

In addition, Brianna showed no concern that Mrs. Walker was standing there listening to all that Brianna told Miss Morgan. Brianna felt out of breath as she blurted out, "Miss Morgan, I heard Melanie on the phone this morning. You won't believe what she said, and I know she was talking to Tuscon, and she asked if Max is still alive." Brianna stopped to take a breath, when Miss Morgan immediately reacted by reaching out and putting her arm around Brianna's shoulders and gently pulling her away from Mrs. Walker's listening ears while quietly whispering to Brianna.

"Don't talk about this with anyone. I'm sure you just imagined hearing that since you were having stomach problems. Telling people this will just start an ugly rumor that will cause confusion. I'm sure you wouldn't want to do that. You need to be very careful about repeating things like that when they're not true. Now just quietly go about your tour of this magnificent place and forget that we ever had this conversation."

Brianna was stunned, but when she looked at Miss Morgan and saw the fake smile on her face, she guessed there was more to this situation than she knew. Miss Morgan had one last comment to Brianna before walking away to join Mrs. Walker while texting on her cell phone, "Remember, Brianna. Don't talk to anyone about this."

CHAPTER 35

There was no problem with the FBI making the connection in Europe with Trenton Bosco. Trenton was only too happy to find out what was really happening to the students in this American group. He had contributed to the investigations of a few other situations here in Europe when the FBI needed help when it was out of their jurisdiction. The FBI in the past had also helped out the European government by finding various criminals who had escaped from Europe to America. It was a comfortable trade-off. Now the FBI had called on Trenton Bosco to get involved. It seemed to him that the job would be easy this time because he had help from Mrs. Vanessa Walker who was travelling with the high school group and was eager to please. She had emailed the trip itinerary to him as he requested by phone so that he would know where the students and chaperones were at all times. He immediately had done his homework on this case with extensive checks into the backgrounds of the students and chaperones and their families.

This job hadn't been difficult so far for Trenton Bosco. Apparently the school board had known which adult on this trip had strong opinions about everything and would be quite willing to cooperate to make herself look like the hero who saved the students and the trip from having a disastrous ending, and had willingly provided the name of Vanessa Walker to the FBI.

No one really knew about Trenton Bosco or the existence of involvement by the Italian government. Even Mrs. Walker didn't know what Trenton Bosco looked like. He could, therefore, blend in like any other tourist in the Piazza San Marco. His eyes were right now on Corrina Morgan. Because he seemed to be interested in only the antiques and history of the place, he actually caught most of what Corrina had said to Brianna. He heard enough to know that for whatever reason, Miss Morgan was trying to keep Brianna from telling anyone about what she had heard Melanie tell someone on the phone this morning. That seemed very strange to Trenton Bosco.

Although he had just begun his investigation into this strange situation, he knew that it seemed highly suspicious that the chaperone in charge of this trip wouldn't find it important that one of the students had reportedly had a phone conversation with one of the missing students, especially about the other missing student. How could you just ignore that and continue exploring this palace like that information didn't matter? Even if it proved to be untrue, wouldn't you at least wonder if you should look into it?

Something wasn't right here and he knew he couldn't just ignore this information. Who was Melanie, anyway, and how would she have knowledge about the missing students that no one else seemed to have?

Trenton was trying to decide if he should approach Corrina Morgan and ask questions or continue to quietly observe to see what would happen next. He didn't have time to think much further because he heard before he saw what was occurring. From somewhere nearby there was a blood-curdling scream. At first he couldn't' tell from what direction it was coming, but when he saw other people running toward the Golden Staircase, according to the signs, he decided to follow them to find out what would cause someone to sound so hysterical.

Although a small crowd was beginning to form, what met his eyes made him realize how serious this was to someone. He was relieved that he was here to see it for himself since he had probably just witnessed what possibly had led to it. Even as he had stood there watching, he had wondered who Corrina Morgan had texted after talking with Brianna. Was this a result of that?

There was Brianna barely hanging on to a railing with a look of terror in her eyes. From the pictures he had received, Trenton identified that it was Austin with Shawna on one side and Melanie on the other side, standing above her. Although Trenton's job was to discreetly investigate this case, he couldn't stand by and watch this girl fall to certain death, which she would if someone didn't grab her quickly. He had no choice. Without further thought he stepped close to the fragile railing and grabbed both of Brianna's wrists. He let go of one of them while wrapping his arm around her waist, and with one movement lifted her back safely onto the steps. She was shaking and crying and having a difficult time standing, but it was Austin who stepped out of the crowd to comfort Brianna. Neither Shawna nor Melanie showed any compassion as they separated from each other and disappeared into the crowd.

Trenton Bosco couldn't say for sure, since he had arrived after the fact, but he felt certain that Shawna or Melanie had everything to do with this. Since it seemed that Brianna was at least temporarily in good hands, he took this opportunity to try to catch up with both girls. With a glance to assure that Brianna seemed calmer, he left as he saw a security guard approaching. He blended in with the crowd that had gathered as it was dispersing and moving on to continue with their tours. He thought as he left the scene, surely these kids aren't so desperate for something that they would attempt to kill someone. In reality, he was just beginning to see how important it must be to one of them.

CHAPTER 36

As Melanie deliberately got lost in the crowd, her thoughts were far away from Piazza San Marco. She could have been anywhere, because in her mind she was already with Tuscon relaxing on a beach somewhere in Italy. This time she would succeed with her plans and make Tuscon happy. Her mission was Austin. She had promised and she always kept her promises. Austin had been a hero for too long. She was tired of hearing about Austin saving them from the kidnappers three years ago. Enough of this hero worship for Austin. She had been there. She could have just as easily saved them all, but she kind of enjoyed being away from everything in that old mansion. It had given her a true sense of belonging and of just being herself. No one seemed to admit it then or afterward, but except for being afraid they might not come out of that kidnapping experience alive, it had not been so terrible. After all, the kidnappers had paid the price for their bad decisions.

As Melanie continued to walk through hallways, she also recalled that Austin had been leaning over touching her hair, one night when she woke up in that remote mansion. He had gotten away with trying to scare her. Melanie was also thinking about the time that Austin had saved Brianna from falling down the stone stairs at the school when she had found the perfect opportunity to push her. And Brianna would have deserved to be hurt for acting so chummy with Melanie's boyfriend. Who did Brianna think she was, moving into the school and making friends with her boyfriend? Now today there was Austin again playing the hero when Brianna could have been out of the picture so easily.

Oh well, she and her boyfriend had broken up anyway, and so Brianna could have had him for all she cared. When he found out that Melanie hadn't made it for cheerleader for next year, he had left her. Not that he admitted leaving her for that reason. He said that it was because Melanie had changed and that she was no longer the sweet, happy person she used to be. Imagine saying that to someone. He had his nerve being rude to her. She just might seek her revenge on him next, but for now it was Austin and then Brianna. Tuscon wanted Austin, and Melanie's goal was to get Tuscon what he wanted. She didn't know why. Tuscon only said they could be together forever if Melanie would help him get Austin.

Melanie did wonder what the episode this morning was about. They had Austin for a brief time this morning right there in the hotel, but then they let him go. What was that all about? Why hadn't they just kept him then? Oh well, maybe later this would all make sense, but for now she had to find a way to punish Brianna for being so smug and get Austin for Tuscon. It was just perfect that they were together.

It shouldn't be impossible to find them now that the crowd was thinning as the sunlight outside was fading. Soon the Piazza would close, and there were many places to hide or trap someone. Now she was on a mission. All she had to do was find Austin again. She had been so close to being able to make him fall by pushing Shawna to hopefully fall into Austin and make him fall down the steps. It hadn't worked out the way she had planned. Instead, in a weird series of events, when Melanie pushed Shawna, it was really just a gentle nudge to her side, Shawna had fallen the other direction and tripped on the steps and strangely enough hit Brianna who was on the steps below them and had fallen through the weak railing.

Even Melanie was surprised by this strange outcome. She hadn't even seen Brianna below them on the steps. What was she doing there anyway? She had almost ended up being a victim without Melanie having to put forth a lot of effort. Would that have been such a strange coincidence? Well, now she had to get it right. Tuscon was waiting, and she was wasting time.

As for kidnapping Max, she guessed that for Tuscon that was all about money. He had said something about ransom money in one of their conversations, but she hadn't paid much attention. She was smart enough to know that when she and Tuscon ended up together, they couldn't just live on love. Relaxing and lying on a beach somewhere would cost money, so Max was their high-priced ticket to the good and beautiful life that Melanie envisioned with Tuscon.

She hadn't heard an amount, but she just bet that a wealthy board member like Max's father would be willing to pay a lot in the hopes of getting his son back. But that was Tuscon's problem to make that happen. Her only assigned task from Tuscon was to get Austin into some place where Tuscon could find him, which also didn't make sense to Melanie. She knew that Tuscon had placed the tracking device into Austin's arm when they were in Milan. It might have felt like a mosquito bite to Austin, but when he came out of that dark alley, he had the tracking device within him.

Now Melanie wasn't a deep thinker, but she had vaguely wondered why Tuscon didn't just do whatever he was going to do to Austin at any time since he knew at every moment where he was. She didn't really understand why she had to help with finding Austin for Tuscon when it was so obvious, but she was only too happy to make Tuscon be pleased with her. After all, Tuscon was obligated to be with Melanie because she knew too much. She thought that no one else knew that Tuscon was behind Max being kidnapped or that Tuscon was even alive, but being naïve had always been one of Melanie's faults.

CHAPTER 37

Although Trenton Bosco had been told that the principal's perception of Vanessa Walker was that she was always interested in other people's business, Trenton was grateful that Mrs. Walker was paying such close attention and was keeping him informed. Her text had told him what she had overheard Brianna tell Miss Morgan. He knew now that somewhere in Italy Tuscon and hopefully Max were still alive. He also knew that Melanie was somehow involved. He hadn't quite figured out what her involvement is, but he knew about the phone conversation that Brianna had heard Melanie having with Tuscon.

By piecing together some facts and through casual discussions today with some of the students about what they thought was going on, Bosco had learned that somehow Miss Morgan seemed to have been instrumental in getting Max kidnapped by sending him up the elevator to her room. He also had derived from the students that Miss Morgan was acting very strange at times, from one extreme to the other between worrying about Tuscon, to almost being frantic, while at other times acting like she didn't care.

From his close proximity to Miss Morgan

when she was talking with Brianna here in the Piazza today, he had heard Miss Morgan caution Brianna not to tell anyone about Melanie and Tuscon being involved and Max possibly still being alive.

Then he felt like his collection of facts and information stopped. He had too many unanswered questions. He speculated that one of the students on the scene when Brianna had fallen was somehow guilty of pushing her, but which one? Austin, Melanie, or Shawna? He knew that there was a lot to solve here, and he knew that the time was quickly passing before John Sterling and his wife arrived in Italy to search for their missing son, Max. Having them there would only complicate his investigation. It was always a challenge to solve a difficult case, but having someone emotionally involved like the parents of a child definitely made his job more problematic.

There was also the immediate concern that some of these high school students right here in the Piazza could be in danger, and not just from whatever was going on with Tuscon and Max, but what seemed to be going on inside of the group. There were some different dynamics that were obvious to him, but not easily explained. Why was the group so fragmented? The group was down to a total of fifteen people without counting Tuscon and Max – five chaperones and ten students. Although this whole place was huge, it seemed odd to him that he had seen very few of them. Where were the other three chaperones, who should be supervising students, and where were the other six National High School students ?

Why hadn't he seen them since they had all

arrived here early this afternoon? Maybe they were all in a safe group together, which would be quite a relief to him. But somehow he didn't quite believe that. Trenton Bosco was not that naïve. He wasn't now, nor had he ever been. That's what made him so good at his job. He knew without a doubt that beyond the obvious concerns of losing students, there was something truly not right about this case. It was something just lurking beneath the surface.

CHAPTER 38

Back in the United States, the high school principal, Barry Pierce, and the former middle school principal, Mark Rollins, were having lunch as they discussed the current situation, as well as what was going on in their own professional and personal lives. While they were sharing thoughts and guesses about what was happening on the field trip, Barry received several texts and phone calls from Superintendent Bernard. It was difficult, in fact, to carry on a meaningful conversation with all the interruptions. Although he felt like he had been only half-listening to Mark, one thing came back into Dr. Pierce's mind as he sat in traffic after leaving Mark Rollins. Something Mark had said stood out about Mark's wife, Liz, who was now on home confinement after spending her time in prison. There was something about a phone call that Mark had overheard his wife having. Something that even to Mark had seemed unusual, but that Barry could now not recall from their conversation.

They had been interrupted so many times that he couldn't quite remember it or put his finger on it. It seemed like it was a name. Some name he had heard before but couldn't remember where. It seemed like it had started with an R. No, maybe an S. No, that wasn't it. Maybe a T. Yes, he was sure it was a T. A name that started with T. However, in all the confusion with the phone calls and trying to get home, he still hadn't found that paper telling him who was on the field trip and where they would be now in Italy. He really needed to find that soon. It just might be important.

CHAPTER 39

Texts seemed to work more consistently than phone calls within the Piazza, and that was how word spread that their group was leaving the Piazza San Marco to go back to the hotel. It was now early evening and they were to get a ride on a gondola back up the Grand Canal. The text was brief, but to the point. Stop what you're doing and leave now. As you would assume, if you got one of those texts, it must have come from a chaperone, and it was time to go. Trenton Bosco, of course, did not get one of those texts, and so he was still left wondering why he wasn't seeing several of the chaperones and students. However, he did see Vanessa Walker ahead of him and hurried to catch up with her.

"Mrs. Walker, you look like you're in a hurry. Are you leaving?"

Vanessa Walker replied, "Yes, we're going back to the hotel now.'

Mr. Bosco felt like he needed more information. "But where is Miss Morgan? You were with her. Where did she go?"

"Mr. Bosco, I'm not her keeper. I don't know where she went after I saw her downstairs. You might need to keep track of her yourself since you seem so interested," as she turned and left the building.

So it was that Trenton Bosco was left with a dilemma. Assume everyone in the group had now boarded a gondola and were gone, or try to determine who might still be here from the high school group. It was obvious that this time he wasn't going to get any assistance from Vanessa Walker. Well, he would just wander around a bit and see if he found anyone from the group.

While Trenton looked down corridors and behind pillars, checking for anyone remaining from the group, Brianna and Austin were walking toward the Triumphal Arch and through the Hall of the Censors that would lead back to the wooden staircase where Brianna had almost gotten seriously injured. Although Brianna felt extremely uneasy going back up those steps, she felt happy and comfortable being with Austin. She knew with him she was safe. It just so happened that they had both received a text from Melanie asking them to meet her in the wooden cell above the staircase. Her text had told them that she wanted to talk with them about something very important that might help them find Max.

Both were slightly hesitant, but also excited about the prospect of helping to find Max. They both silently thought, nothing can happen here. Although Brianna knew that Melanie might somehow be involved with Tuscon, she also believed that Austin was brave and would be able to deal with whatever situation would arise from this meeting with Melanie.

Now as they walked together and neared the

top of the steps, getting closer to the old wooden cell, they could see Melanie standing there looking toward them with that angelic smile on her face. That smile had fooled so many people, and here Melanie was again in all her radiance waiting to talk with them with that smile on her face. She turned as they grew closer to her and walked into the cell beckoning them to enter and sit on the wooden bench inside, with the warning, "We don't want anyone to hear us talking."

So it was just that simple to get them inside of the cell with only one weak light in the back corner. She started the conversation with an explanation, "I was hoping that together we could save Max. I think I know who has him and how we can get him back, but you've got to promise me that it will be our secret. If anyone else finds out where he is, they might come after us."

As planned, the conversation got them interested enough that Melanie felt quite content sitting down with them on the bench to tell them more. She was making up most of this, but Austin was so anxious to help that he couldn't keep from listening with the hope that he could find Tuscon and Max. As the three sat there they became vaguely aware that someone was walking up the stairs that would lead the person right to the cell where they sat. Austin and Brianna assumed in their subconscious that it was a security guard who would tell them they needed to leave now. In their minds, they needed to hear all that Melanie had to say, so they were not in a hurry to leave.

Melanie, on the other hand, assumed that it was

Tuscon coming toward them and that he would be grateful to see that she had Austin right there for him to take with him. Melanie again briefly wondered what Tuscon wanted Austin for, but it didn't really matter to her why. Brianna was just there so that Melanie could finish the job right this time that she had failed to do correctly the other two times. This time she would make sure that Brianna fell down the stairs and would never get up again.

The sound of walking footsteps came closer while the shadow outside the cell doorway became a human shape. Both Austin and Brianna gasped as Tuscon appeared in the dim light, while Melanie ran toward the door to greet him, anticipating that she would throw herself into his arms while he would smile at her and tell her how happy he was to see her and how proud he was of her for doing such a wonderful job of getting Austin there for him.

Instead, what happened left Melanie screaming, 'Tuscon, what are you doing? It's me, Melanie. I did what you wanted. I have Austin. He's right here. You can get him right now!" Tuscon was not listening. He had slammed the door shut and the sound of a deadbolt being locked could be heard.

"Tuscon, let me out!"

Silence on the outside of the door, and then Tuscon's voice saying, "Melanie, did you really think I would let you live when you know what I'm doing? Surely you didn't believe that you and I would end up together. I had no intention of sharing any ransom money with you. It's never been about you. It's about me getting back at Austin. Now, this is what needs to happen. I'm going to open the door just long enough for Austin to come out here. Then the door will be closed and locked until I come back for you two. Conveniently, not even texts work in this cell, so don't bother trying to get someone here to help you. You two will also be going into the sea after I come back. I can't take a chance on you two talking about what you know. Meantime, Austin and I will be on our merry way out to the sea. He won't survive the swim in the Adriatic Sea. He'll just disappear and never be found. Swimming in the ocean in the dark can be very dangerous, so Austin surviving that is highly unlikely. As for Max, I should have the money soon that I've demanded for his safe return. His parents will find him in the basement of the hotel where we stayed in Milan. You would have thought someone would have looked for him down there in the boiler room. At this point I don't really care what happens to him as long as I get the ten million dollars.

The door slowly opened and Tuscon stood with a knife pointed at Austin. "Walk this direction very slowly. I'm going to put handcuffs on you and then you're coming with me. Don't try to do anything foolish that you will definitely regret. You see, getting rid of you right now would be so much easier than walking you to the sea anyhow. So don't tempt me. By the way, I'm curious. Have you ever tried swimming in handcuffs with your arms behind your back? That should be interesting to watch, but it's so dark outside, it will not be easy to see. It shouldn't take long to know the ending to this story."

With that said, Tuscon clasped the handcuffs,

closed the door, threw the bolt to lock it, and pulled Austin by the elbow as they started toward the passage that would lead to the sea. While they made their way in the semidarkness, Melanie could be heard screaming, "Tuscon, don't leave me! You promised that we'd be together. How could you do this to me?"

Tuscon mumbled as he led Austin, "Did she really think I would share all that money with her?"

Trenton Bosco thought, as he followed them in the shadows, do you really think you're ever going to see that money?

CHAPTER 40

Bosco followed at a safe distance, while making sure not to let Austin out of his sight. Tuscon had sounded completely unstable, and would therefore be unpredictable as he led his victim to certain death if Trenton lost track of them. Now outside of the space around the cell, as he glided from one shadow to the next, he texted the Italian police for back up, hoping that they would reach them before Tuscon carried out his plan. Trenton also silently hoped that Austin didn't try to do something foolish like physically attempt to overpower Tuscon. That wouldn't be possible in handcuffs, so just keep walking with Tuscon and don't try to be a hero now. But Trenton Bosco didn't know Austin well, and there was a very good chance that he couldn't even imagine what Austin was capable of.

Bosco was so occupied with wanting Austin to just keep moving slowly to buy more time until additional help could arrive, that at first he didn't believe what he was seeing. There before him in the dim light he watched as Austin tried to pull his arm from Tuscon's grasp. They struggled in the grayness, but the glint of the knife was easily seen at even the distance from where Bosco was as he was slinking toward them. He heard the result of Austin's struggles before he saw it. Austin's groan of pain was unmistakable, and Tuscon's laugh was clearly heard above the sound of the nearby ocean waves crashing on the shore. Austin didn't make it to the edge of the water before collapsing on the beach. That didn't stop Tuscon from dragging Austin toward the water as he yelled, "I'm not taking any chances on you surviving the stabbing. You're going into the ocean just as I had planned," as he half carried Austin closer to the water's edge.

Trenton Bosco knew that even without back-up, he would have to do something now because once Tuscon got Austin into the dark water the waves would quickly carry him out to sea. It was now or never. He ran toward the dark forms in silence, taking Tuscon by surprise as he leapt onto Tuscon's back while trying to grab the knife before Tuscon used it to stab Austin again. Not sure where to grab, he felt the blade slice his hand. But the quiet attack had taken Tuscon completely by surprise. As he struggled against this unknown assailant, he fell onto the sand and rocks while screaming into the night, "No! Austin is mine. You can't have him!" as the sound of sirens began filling the silence of the night.

CHAPTER 41

It was obvious to the police officers that this young man was totally out of control. Even in the interrogation room, Tuscon had to be handcuffed and carefully secured with a guard standing nearby. His rage could be physically felt in the small space. His face was contorted into such anger that his words were slurred and blood dripped from his lips from biting his tongue in his uncontrollable rage.

That didn't stop Bosco and the sergeant in charge from bombarding him with questions. Trenton Bosco had been close enough to the wooden cell, before Tuscon took Austin, that he had heard him tell the students where Max was being held. Hopefully he would be found safe and sound before his parents landed in Italy.

There was so much more to find out. Austin had been taken unconscious to the nearest hospital. He had lost a lot of blood from the wound in his back. Surgery would provide the information that would tell the doctors if vital organs had been damaged and how long he would have to recover before leaving Italy.

But there was so much more to find out, and right now Tuscon wasn't making it easy to get answers. He had made it known on his ride to the police station that Corrina Morgan needed to be brought to the police station. Assuming it was because she was the head chaperone for the field trip, they were completely unprepared for what happened when Miss Morgan entered the space where Tuscon was handcuffed.

In his rage, Tuscon fought the officers holding him while screaming at Miss Morgan as she backed away as much as the confined space would allow. Apparently the police had not told her that Tuscon had been found, so her reaction was at first shock to see him there, and then fear. Fear of Tuscon or fear of something else. What was really going on here?

The police imagined the typical reaction of a teacher who thought she had lost a student. Shouldn't she be thrilled that he was there and alive? That would be the expected response, but that's not what they were seeing. Instead, Tuscon was struggling to get away from his guards while physically and verbally lashing out at Corrina Morgan. His words were at first unclear, but then began to make more frightening sense.

"How could you mess this up so much? We had it all worked out. Everything was planned."

At first Miss Morgan pretended to not know what Tuscon was talking about, as she tried to act like he was speaking nonsense in his rage. But his next words were undoubtedly very clear to all within hearing.

"I asked you to plan this trip for me, but now there won't be any money for either of us. It would have all been so perfect."

CHAPTER 42

Trenton Bosco had a lot to decipher. There were still some unanswered questions. Interviewing and questioning provided him with enough facts that he finally could begin to put the pieces of the puzzle together even as he helped to make arrangements for ending this field trip and sending everyone back home to the United States. They wouldn't get to see Rome this time.

He started with the obvious question. Why had Corrina Morgan agreed to plan this trip? Tuscon had approached her in linguistics class with an innocent question. Wouldn't it be fun to take a field trip to Italy so we can practice all this stuff that you have taught us? So the seed was planted and took root. Now the question, why did Tuscon want the trip? Was it just to have a good time? No. For Tuscon it was never about having a good time. Apparently it was all about greed and finding an easy way to have an unlimited amount of money. Along the way, he began talking with Miss Morgan about his plan, or at least part of his plan. He never really told her how it would happen, but he did promise her that if she got the principal to agree to allow them to go on a trip to Italy, he would share millions of dollars with her.

Sadly, Miss Morgan had agreed to that for one reason, her father needed money to cover his medical expenses. Corrina Morgan always tried to help her parents, but this time she didn't help them in the right way, and ended up causing them and a lot of people unnecessary anguish. She didn't know what Tuscon's plans were, but she did know that her stress started from the first day of the trip in the airport. From the beginning, it appeared that Tuscon was unpredictable. She couldn't tell whether his disappearance was part of the act or if he planned to skip out on their plan to get rich. She had been frantic to find him for obvious reasons. He had convinced her to go along with a plan, but had never told her how it would happen.

Besides Tuscon's disappearance from the hotel, Corrina's first real indication of something happening was being followed in Milan and threatened as she was told what to do. She had experienced some slight guilt over Max being a possible victim, but not enough guilt to stop the process once it had started. Greed had taken over Corrina's mind regardless of the reason for doing it.

It was Tuscon in one of his many disguises and invented accent who had followed Miss Morgan in Milan and told her what to do. He had acted alone until he asked the blond and her boyfriend in a bar, after giving them a few free drinks, to show up in the hotel when he contacted them to pull Austin out of the hallway. They had no idea why Tuscon wanted the kid to be pulled aside, but while they had Austin in the room in the hotel they had received a call on their cell phone that told them to let him go, with the only explanation being that he couldn't do anything now because it was too soon. During that time, he had put a plan in place to use Melanie who was only too happy to help him. She would willingly get Austin for Tuscon so that he could easily dispose of Austin into the sea where no one would know to look for him. And although Melanie thought Tuscon was going to share millions with her, he never had any intention of giving Melanie anything except a quick but painful fall from the clock tower in Venice at the Piazza San Marco or a permanent swim in the Adriatic Sea.

But there was only one important unanswered question left for Trenton Bosco to feel satisfied that he had solved this mystery. Why did Tuscon want Austin dead? Surely this was not jealousy over Austin being a hero. Tuscon didn't have any reason to even care about the school kidnapping three years ago. Or did he? Bosco was still looking for the solution to this puzzle.

CHAPTER 43

In the United States at this moment, Dr. Barry Pierce found in a pile on his desk that elusive piece of paper that listed the chaperones and students of the trip to Italy, as well as the itinerary. Now to call Mark Rollins to find out what he had been talking about at lunch. Mark Rollins was thankfully at home. Dr. Pierce was anxious to be able to tell something positive to the FBI connection that was in Italy, Trenton Bosco, to help him figure out what was going on with this field trip with missing students.

"Mark, this is Barry Pierce. Hey, I wanted to talk with you again about what we were discussing at lunch today. To be honest, I was a little preoccupied and I missed something that you were telling me about a phone call you overheard your wife, Liz, having with someone. I apologize for that, but I was hoping you wouldn't mind telling me again what that was about."

It was obvious that Mark Rollins was feeling even more emotional about this topic than he had been at lunch. Reality had sunk in and he would feel relieved to discuss it with a friend.

"Barry, I overheard my wife talking on the phone last night. She's on home confinement after being in prison, and since she's home all the time, she talks on the phone a lot. I've even heard her talk to that woman, Jo Lee, who helped kidnap the students from my school. How could she do that? But this conversation I heard last night was different. She was talking to this person about revenge being sweet and how happy she would be after he had taken care of someone named Austin because she said he had caused her to go to prison after the school kidnapping. I know it sounds weird, but I know she said to the person she was talking to that she was so proud to have him for a son even if her husband never knew about him. Can you imagine, Barry? She's talking about me not knowing about something that important."

Barry heard Mark finally take a breath before continuing. "I'm just finding out that my wife had a baby that she gave away before I ever met her? But she talked to this person like she talked to him all the time. Like they were really comfortable with each other. From the sound of their conversation it seems like she has probably been in contact with him all his life, and I'm just finding out about him now. What kind of person hides something like that from her husband?"

Barry didn't want to be cruel to his friend, but he wanted to say to Mark that he believes that the same kind of person who hides having a child is the same kind of person who gambles her husband's salary and sells information to kidnappers and causes her husband to lose his job and career, but Barry was trying hard to be supportive as he sat listening and looking at the piece of paper lying in front of him on his desk that listed names and places in Italy.

"Mark, I know how upsetting this must be to you, but there's something I have to ask you. Do you know the name of your wife's son?"

Mark softly replied, "Yes. It's Tuscon."

Epilogue

Max was found by the police exactly where Tuscon said he would be. He was dehydrated and feverish, and extremely hungry, but alive and ecstatic to be reunited with his parents. They would help to get Max well and tour some of the cities in Italy before returning to the United States.

Liz Rollins wouldn't get off as easy this time. Conspiracy to attempted murder of Austin would carry a much stiffer prison sentence. Because she had violated her parole, she would undoubtedly spend the rest of her life in prison. Mark Rollins didn't lose much sleep over her treachery this time. He planned to eventually move to another state and begin to apply for jobs as a principal.

Tuscon had a plan all along from the time Miss Morgan agreed to take the trip. Once he was on his way to Italy, he had tried to get away from Miss Morgan as early as the first flight by pretending to be sick and by disguising himself, but she had made such an uproar on the plane that he had decided to wait and make another, less obvious, plan. Now back in the United States, he would be tried as an adult for threatening and attempting murder, kidnapping, conspiracy, fraud, and extortion, although the ten-million-dollar ransom was never paid. He would never see his mother again since they would be in different prisons.

As for Corrina Morgan, just as Tuscon had predicted, she did lose her job as a teacher. She is still on bond awaiting trial to determine the extent of her involvement and her punishment. While she was not directly involved with the actual threat of murder of Austin, she was knowledgeable of Max's kidnapping, as well as participating in the conspiracy with Tuscon of extortion for money for Max's return. She also conspired with Tuscon to plan the trip, at first innocently, and then with an illegal and unethical purpose. She still had mixed feelings about her role in the misadventure. While she would probably swear to tell the truth on the stand, she wasn't sure anymore what the truth was. She would begin receiving therapy while she awaited trial. Her parents were safe, but her father still had medical needs. She really had nothing to do with the cake. It was just planned by Tuscon as a distraction with a dose of a drug to induce vomiting to cause them all to have stomach problems, giving Tuscon more time to get the ransom money.

Dr. Barry Pierce immediately contacted Trenton Bosco after talking to Mark Rollins and hearing the name Tuscon. Mr. Bosco had put most of the pieces together, but knowing why Tuscon was out to kill Austin was the last piece that completed the puzzle. Liz Rollins may have been out for sweet revenge, but using her own son, Tuscon, to get that revenge led to her losing her son forever. Maybe finally Liz Rollins would realize that crime doesn't pay.

Made in the USA
Middletown, DE
03 April 2016